TONY SPARANDARA

FISH

Copyright © 2015

All rights reserved. No part of this book may be reproduced or transmitted in any form or by any means, electronic or mechanical, including photocopying, recording, or by any information storage and retrieval system, without the written permission of the author, except where permitted by law.

Illustrations by Olivia Warnecke
Book layout and design by Michael Sparandara

For Melanie Sparandara:
Without you, there would be no story.

FISH

Chapter 1

"Run, goddamnit! You run like my grandmother – and she's been dead for twenty years."

Coach Angelo Fischetti, everybody called him "Fish," was in rare form today. Usually the boys ran like other deceased family members, but he hadn't pulled grandma out of his ass in quite a while. His father was one of his favorites, but he was only dead nine years and presumably still in much better shape than the long-departed Nana. They weren't even running fast enough for Pops today.

Of course, the fact that they were on quarter number nine, in a set of twelve, trying to run each one really fast on short recovery, had something to do with their distress. Oh yeah, it was also forty-one degrees and raining, on March the eighth, the FIRST day of spring track practice.

"Carbone, you're slow as shit. It's like watching molasses in January - going uphill. Can't you run any faster? You're supposed to be the captain."

The disparaging similes continued – paired with the occasional cliché.

"It's cold, Fish - muscle-pulling weather," Frankie Carbone replied.

"Then you have absolutely nothing to worry about."

"For real, coach. It's Day One; we got time."

"Time waits for no man," Fish decided. And with that, he turned his back and walked across the football field to yell at the long jumpers, who were trying to get their steps into the teeth of a twenty mile-per-hour headwind.

Cameron Nelson, the usually jovial Jamaican quarter-miler, turned to his captain. His chest was heaving and his eyes were rolling wildly in his head.

"Frankie, mon, me caan do dis no more. Dis man Fish wah kill uz all."

"Stop bein' a wuss...three more," Frankie answered. "I got this one; you get the next, and Russ takes the last. Fish hasn't killed anybody, yet."

"Not that we know of," said Russell.

"Ready, go," Carbone yelled, and they were off on quarter number ten - only two more to go.

Chapter 2

Every day after practice, Fish and his assistant coaches sat in the cramped Coaches Office shootin' the breeze. They commented on practice, society at large, and anything else that crossed their minds. All three of the assistants had been part of the program for years, and they were all good guys who knew their stuff. Josh Olson, a laid-back history teacher and former college decathlete, handled the hurdlers, high jumpers, and pole vaulters. Gym teacher Joe Pellegrino, a grizzled 250-pound former shot putter and power lifter, instructed the throwers, and Kevin Cahill, a retired local cop who still held the school's cross country record, trained the distance runners. Fish concentrated on the sprinters and horizontal jumpers, but he had a hand in everything.

"Anybody see anything good today?" Fish asked hopefully.

"Hell no," Cahill, the resident cynic, responded. "The distance runners are slow, lazy, and out of shape. Outside of that they're fine. The only one with any actual talent is Glick, and he's totally insane."

"Does he still stop running for no apparent reason?" Fish inquired.

"Yeah and it's getting worse. Today he stopped in the middle of the third rep. When I asked him what was up, he said he felt 'too good.' He's a total wack job."

"He just needs to get laid," Coach Pell suggested. That was pretty much Pell's solution to all of life's minor problems.

"That might actually work, but first he'd have to talk to a girl," Cahill countered.

"That could be arranged."

"I mean without payin' for it."

"Hold off on the pimpin'," Fish cut in. "Kev, you know him better than anyone else. In twenty-five words or less, what's his problem?"

"He's afraid to do well," the distance coach said. "His whole life he's been the smallest and the weakest, the runt of the litter. The kids tease him unmercifully; geez, even some of his teachers tease him. Now that there's something he's actually good at, he can't handle it. Every time he's about to do well, he pulls back. That's why he kept finishing second and third in all those races last year; he's afraid to win. The question is, how do we make him unafraid?"

"Thank you, Doctor Fraud," Pell growled, "and that was way more than twenty-five words. I still vote for gettin' him laid."

"Well, Freud's work did have a certain, ahem, sexual aspect to it," Cahill noted.

"Yo!" Olson protested. "Are we track coaches or a bunch of half-assed shrinks?"

"Ah," Fish muttered, "they're basically the same thing."

Chapter 3

Westfield had withered – both the town and its high school. After Morgan Mills, *"For All Your Cotton Needs,"* had moved down to Georgia twenty years ago, the once vibrant village had gone downhill in a hurry. Abandoned stores now dotted the business district and foreclosure signs had sprung up like weeds. Many of the young families, or at least the ones that could afford to, had left town because there were no jobs and nothing to do. In fact, the town's main thoroughfare, which in rosier times had been a bustling hub of shopping and socializing, was now known as Boredway. And, with unemployment soaring and money tight, petty crime was up, too.

Built in the late 1950's, the dirty red brick high school symbolized the town. Its ancient roof leaked with every rain and its golden dome had long since tarnished to a grimy green. Once the pride of the district's six public schools, a series of failed budgets and years of austerity had condemned it to its current sorry state.

The student body had changed, too. Years ago, Westfield had been one of the county's top high schools, but now it had settled comfortably into the lowest quarter of the academic ranks. The best students had fled to private and parochial schools, and the children of immigrants had taken their places. Spanish, Russian, Korean, and a dozen other languages filled the school's hallways.

There were still a few holdouts, though. Some of the working class whites that had gone to the school for generations were still around, and the handful of black families that used to provide domestic help for the rich people who lived down by the water also remained.

Fish had been there for all of it. Starting out as a brash twenty-one-year-old right out of college, he had taught in the school's English Department for thirty-six years, eventually rising to the rank of chairman. In that time, he'd made a million friends and only a slightly smaller number of enemies. And, while his fearlessness in trying to do the right thing had won him a legion of admirers, it had also bruised more than a few egos. Nevertheless, at the age of fifty-seven he wasn't about to undergo any miraculous transformation. As a wise man once said, "When people get older they don't change; they just get better at what they are."

Chapter 4

The captain of the moribund Westfield Wildcats, by the unanimous vote of his teammates, was "Little Frankie Carbone." He was a skinny little freshman when he first met Fish and he was a skinny little senior now.

In Frankie's own words, "I was just hangin' around after school one day, minding my own business where cross country practice was going on. That was my first mistake."

"Can I help you son?" a surprisingly friendly voice boomed. "You look a little lost."

"Uh, no, that's OK, thanks," Frankie said. "I'm just chillin'."

"Well, why don't you come over here and chill with us?" The team was stretching now. "We're always lookin' for a few good men."

"No thanks… really. I'm cool."

The guy talking sounded like that Marine Corps recruiter on TV, and Frankie didn't want any part of the military, him, or his team. He just wanted to hang out on a warm September afternoon.

Fish persisted, though.

"Listen, you really can't stay here unless you're on the team," he whispered under his breath. "You know what I mean? There's some rule about insurance or something."

That was a crock – the first of many Fish would offer. Fish is a good guy, really good, but he's kinda loose with the truth. He's such a good liar that nobody can ever be sure if he believes what he's sayin' or if he just wants people to believe it. How could a guy get hurt watching other guys run? There was no way.

"So, if you wanna stick around, you'd better get out here," Fish continued.

Frankie was only fourteen at the time; what the hell did he know? Slowly, he ambled onto the track and started stretching. Although he didn't realize it at the time, both his track career and his relationship with Fish had officially begun.

Chapter 5

Another reason why the Fish-Frankie relationship was complicated was that Fish had quickly and quietly insinuated himself into the Carbones' lives.

Frankie's mom was currently working as a waitress over at Big Mario's Ristorante, which was by far the best eating joint in town. And, the reason she was working there at all was because Fish got her the job.

After Frankie's father, the late Joey Carbone, died in a construction accident a couple of years ago, his wife and only child found themselves in some serious financial trouble. They didn't get much of a settlement from the insurance company, and the rent on the house they were living in was way too high to manage. So, they had moved to the little one-bedroom apartment that they were in now. It was in a shabby old section of town called "The Flats" because the neighborhood sits down low between two small hills, but everybody who lived there called it "The Flats" because they were all pretty much flat broke. Even with the lower rent, making ends meet was still tough because Mrs. Carbone only worked part-time as a receptionist at the local health clinic; they had relied totally on Frankie's dad to pay the bills.

Around this time, Fish decided to get involved.

"How's that new apartment workin' out, Frankie boy?" he asked one day after practice.

He already knew the answer because he knew everything that went on in Westfield, but he asked anyway.

"All right, I guess, Frankie answered. "It's a little cramped, but…it's… uh…OK."

Fish picked up on the kid's hesitation right away.

"How's the rent? I know your mom's workin' down at the clinic."

"Actually, it's a little tough for us. She's tryin' to get some more hours, but there's too many people working there. I think I might have to stop running, too. I need to get a part-time job and help out."

"Hmm…," Fish didn't say anything for about a minute. "Let me think about that; we sure don't want to lose a guy like you."

That made Frankie feel a little better, but what could Fish do? He was only a teacher; he couldn't just snap his fingers and find his mom a better job.

Fish continued to stare off into the distance and rubbed his chin for a while. Then he turned back around.

"Your mom ever done any waitressing?" he asked.
"Not that I know of," Frankie answered.

"Well, it's not exactly brain surgery, and it'll sure as hell pay better than the clinic. Why don't you ask her if she's interested? I know this guy."

Fish always "knew a guy," and if this job paid better than the clinic then Frankie's mom would definitely be interested. After the kid filled her in at supper, she gave him the OK to have Fish make the call.

The guy Fish knew was Big Mario Iannucci, so named because of his enormous size and to distinguish him from his two cousins, both also named Mario Iannucci, who lived in town as well. Big Mario had been this legendary football player and trackman at Westfield back in the day, and Fish had tutored him in English, a necessary language skill since Mario and his family had only recently arrived from Calabria. Fish had taught him for free of course, what he called the "Westfield Rate," because Big Mario's parents didn't have any money, and then he had coached the kid to state titles in the shot put and discus. After Big Mario returned from Michigan State, where he'd been an All-Big Ten defensive end before blowing out his knee, he settled back in Westfield and opened his eatery.

Two days after Fish called him, Mrs. Carbone was waiting tables at the restaurant.

Chapter 6

Fish bolted into his house – late as usual. Dinner was supposed to be at six, but in truth it was whenever practice and its accompanying post-mortem ended. Fish's wife, the long-suffering Nina Fischetti, had long ago given up any hope of keeping her husband on a regular schedule. She was a schoolteacher, too – Catholic elementary division - who managed in her spare time to organize their three kids' schedules, cook mouth-watering meals, and keep a neat home, all in the name of familial peace. Being Fish's wife took patience – lots of it – and Nina had that in abundance. Too many of her friends' marriages had ended badly, and she had long ago vowed that it would never happen to her. If it took some flexibility and creativity to deal with her husband's long hours and missed meals, so be it. Being married to Fish, no one dared call him Angelo except his mother, was a trip for sure, but the man did have a good heart - even if he kept it very well hidden.

The couple had been married for almost thirty years and had three children. The oldest, AJ, for Angelo, Jr., was nineteen and a sophomore in college. The spitting image of his father, he marched to the beat of a drum that no else in his family heard or even knew existed. As the Fischetti's resident free spirit, he was majoring in medieval architecture at SUNY Albany, styled his shoulder-length black hair into a long ponytail, and wore clothes salvaged from local thrift shops. His current passion in life was as the front man for the head bangin' "Septic Dwarves," a local garage band whose name told you all you needed to know about their music.

Child number two was their fourteen-year-old daughter Maria, a freshman at Westfield. Distancing herself from her older brother as much as possible, she was the valedictorian of her class, the three-term grade president, and a weekend volunteer at the local animal shelter. She had already informed her parents of her intention to graduate from Yale, go to law school, and eventually enter politics. The goal of becoming America's first female president was not completely out of the question. Fish had decided that he wouldn't be retiring any time soon.

The baby of the bunch was eleven-year-old Matthew, Matty for short. Tall for his age, with dirty blonde hair and piercing blue-gray eyes, he defied the Italian stereotype. He was quiet to a fault and more than content to let his gregarious older siblings dominate the conversations at dinner and elsewhere, while he calmly sat back and surveyed things. His twin obsessions were playing fantasy computer games and shooting things with his brand new WHAM-O slingshot, a Christmas gift that Fish's wife had been firmly against – particularly for a sixth-grader.

"I had a slingshot when I was his age," Fish had argued. "Everybody had one. Nothin' wrong with it."

"That was fifty years ago," Nina replied. "You probably had a crew cut and wore little wife-beaters, too."

"I did. Nothin' wrong with those, either. And, I didn't have a fancy computer keepin' me inside all day."

"That's because there were no computers back then."

"That's what I'm sayin'," Fish answered.

"What are you saying?" his wife asked. "You're not making any sense."

"Yeah I am. I'm making plenty of sense," Fish decided. "Listen, did you have a slingshot when you were a kid?"

"No…of course not," his wife replied.

"What did you have, dolls and stuff?"

"Yes… and a bike and a little red wagon."

"See, that's what I'm talkin' about."

"What are you talking about?"

"Matty's a boy; that's why he's got a slingshot. It's a guy thing."

Nina just shook her head sadly and finished drying the dishes.

Chapter 7

"We're not good enough," Fish began.

The coaches were into their daily bull session, and the headman wasn't smiling.

"We don't have enough studs, not for this league anyway. Greenmont is loaded – like always, and Kingsbridge is even better. They have those twins from Yugoslavia or some goddamn place who win about five events each. Franklin

North is pretty good, too. We're no better than fourth - at best."

Fish was exaggerating, but not by much. Yugoslavia hadn't been a country for about twenty years, and league rules prohibited an athlete from competing in more than three events, but his point was well taken. The Danicic twins were terrific athletes, and the three teams he mentioned were all very good. Westfield hadn't won a track title in forever, and it didn't look like they'd be hanging a banner any time soon.

"There have to be some athletes we're missing," Fish continued. "Joe, how about your gym classes? There must be somebody in there."

Pell rubbed the perpetual stubble on his chin. "Most of the good athletes play lacrosse in the spring, and the ones that don't play baseball, or have jobs, or go home and whack off. Not too many kids want to hang around for two hours after school running around a track."

"He's right," Cahill added. "We're The Legion of the Lost; we get all the rejects. Give us your tired, your poor, your huddled masses yearning to run track. How many real athletes do we have?"

"Not enough," Pell agreed.

"There's Carbone," Olson offered.

"Heart of a lion, body of a Chihuahua," Fish snarled. "Not much of a market for midget hurdlers."

"How about Green? He's fast as hell - at least for the short stuff."

"If you point him in the right direction, maybe; but he's the dumbest son-of-a-bitch I've ever seen. He wanders around like a fart in a windstorm. He can't even stay in his own lane. How the hell is he gonna beat anybody?"

"Jenkins? He's tall at least."

"Length – no strength."

"Simmons? McDermott?"

"No! And, a really big no! Fat distance runners don't usually fare very well. We need new blood, and we need it fast; our first meet is in two weeks."

Chapter 8

And so, the recruiting process began. No stone was left unturned, and what eventually crawled out from under one of those rocks proved to be very interesting.

Fish wandered into the cafeteria at the start of fifth period one day looking to grab a snack for practice. He was always munching on something, which never made his runners feel any better when they were ready to puke their guts out after a hard workout, but he claimed he needed it "to keep up the old energy."

Silently casing the joint, he spotted a very large and extremely quiet youngster sitting alone at a corner table. Fish sauntered over, pulled out a chair, and sat down across from him.

"What's your name, son? I haven't seen you around." Fish might not have seen this kid around, but he would have said that anyway, "just to break the ice."

"Oscar," the teen mumbled softly.

"Oscar what? The Grouch?"

"Nah," the kid smiled shyly. "Oscar Amaya "

"What grade are you in, Oscar Amaya?"

"Twelfth"

"Hmm, well, you look like an athlete Oscar. You play any sports?"

"Football"

In truth, Oscar Amaya didn't look like an athlete at all; he looked like a giant pear. He had a round baby face plastered on a smallish head that sat on surprisingly narrow shoulders for a boy his size. But, those shoulders sloped pyramid-like to a barrel chest and a triple-X waist. A pair of tree trunks that passed for legs completed the widescreen picture.

Oscar was on the football team all right, but he only served as a tackling dummy at practice. In his two years on the varsity he had never gotten into a game. However, since he stood well over six feet tall and weighed in at better than 300 pounds, his place on the squad was assured.

Surprisingly, he seemed somewhat intrigued when Fish floated the idea of coming out for track.

"We'll make him a shot putter," Fish announced to his assistants at their daily briefing. "Joe, you work with him; you'll get him going."

"Oscar? Oscar Amaya? He's the Pillsbury Doughboy," Pell protested. "He's a hundred pounds overweight with no muscles at all. I'll bet you he can't bench a hundred."

"It's not a weightlifting contest; it's track and field. You're a great coach; you'll develop him."

"Don't flatter me, Fish. I'm not that great - nobody is. I'd rather work with what we got, little as it is."

"You can work with the other guys, too, but Oscar's got potential."

"Potential? For what? Competitive eating? We should put him in that Nathan's hot dog contest; he'd win it easy.

Did you know he's majoring in lunch? Seriously, he has it for three periods - four, five, and six."

"Go see his counselor tomorrow. Get him some more classes. Maybe that dance class they have period five is open. We'll 'Dance His Ass Off.' And, I can stick him in an extra English class period four. That'll keep him out of the cafeteria."

"This isn't gonna work," Pell protested.

"Maybe not, but we have to try. And Joe, keep him away from the Twinkies - he's big enough already."

Chapter 9

Practice today was brutal. After a two-mile warm-up, the team broke into their event groups. The coaches, in a desperate attempt to make up for a lack of talent, were determined to out condition their opponents. It was a plan that might have worked, except for the fact that nobody was buying in. Cam was the first to crack.

"Frankie mon, dis rass coach ya maaad; em tink wi a don-kees." His soft Caribbean accent turned shrill. "Mi shoulda stay a Ja-mai-ca, mon, a leas di weather warmer doun deh. An, dem dash peeple like Fish ina jail."

"We can do it," Frankie countered. "We're halfway done."

"A dat mi a say, on-lee afway, we hav a whole heep lef."

Cam did have a point. They had already run three 600's and three 300's, and there were still a bunch left.

"What do you want to do?" Frankie asked.

"Ga home a mi yard!" Cam replied. "Ga home an get ina mi wahm bed. An, mi no wa no mad coach ah bark afta mi."

Russell Grimaldi, another quarter man, chimed in.

"You know Cam's right; this sucks! You're the captain; Fish actually likes you. Why don't you talk to him?"

"Fish isn't usually real eager to hear my suggestions," Frankie answered. "I don't think it'll help."

"Mi no care," Cam countered. "Mi legs dem mash up; mi wa go home a mi yard.

"Me, too," added Russ. And with that, the disgruntled duo trudged off the track and headed towards the locker room.

Frankie struggled through the rest of the workout alone. He had to admit though, the guys were right – this wasn't any fun at all.

Chapter 10

The two AWOL quarter milers returned to practice the next day, and it was Saint Patty's Day to boot, but the coaches, including Cahill who was aggressively Irish, weren't in a celebratory mood.

"You know you're gonna have a mutiny on your hands," Cahill began as soon as the coaches had settled into their chairs.

"Over what?" Fish queried. "Everything's fine."

"Half the team is ready to quit. You're killin' 'em."

"They have to get in shape. They're not even close yet."

"There's not gonna be anybody left to get in shape," Cahill went on. "Did you know Cam and Russell bugged out early yesterday? And, two of the distance guys just begged off with phantom injuries."

"How about Glick? He didn't stop, did he?"

"No, he didn't," Cahill continued. "Because he had a sore throat and said he felt lousy. If he felt good, he would've stopped. He's nuts! Don't you remember?"

"Yeah, I do, unfortunately. So, what's the answer?"

"Ease up. Make it fun. At least we'll keep some guys on the team."

"But we won't beat anybody."

"We're not gonna beat anybody with no team. We need more guys, not less."

Fish turned to Pell and Olson. "What do you guys think?"

"Kev's right," Pell offered. "Even the weight guys are hurtin', and they don't run. They're liftin' every day, Monday-Wednesday-Friday upper body, heavy, and Tuesday-Thursday-Saturday legs. And, they're throwin' three times a week, too. They could use a break."

"How does the big boy look?"

"Oscar? Like Baby Huey. He throws the shot like a baseball; he doesn't get the put part yet."

"How about the disc?"

"He thinks it's a Frisbee. He threw it backhanded yesterday."

"And his weight?"

"Up - from 330 to 338."

"When he gets to 350, sell. Josh, how about you? Give me something for Christ's sake."

"I wish I could. The vaulters look all right, but it's always too cold and rainy to jump. They're getting sick of running around doing planting drills. The high jumpers stink; nobody can clear more than five-four. And the hurdlers, except for Carbone, are awfully raw; he's going to have to carry the load. We could really use a good combo guy behind him."

"Well, that pretty much sums it up," Fish concluded. "We still suck and the season is upon us. I'll think about how to have more fun. You guys figure out how to get us some more athletes."

Chapter 11

Saturday practices were different. They started at ten o'clock so the guys could sleep a little after a rough Friday night, and the workouts weren't rushed; they could end whenever. There was a bad omen today, though. As soon as the runners hit the track to warm-up, Rocky was there. Rocky was Fish's beloved black lab, and his presence at practice meant only two things: there was some hard running in store, and Rocky was going to chase people around the track. Now Rocky was a friendly dog; thank God he didn't bite. But he was playful, too, a little too playful when exhausted runners were trying to finish up strong. Fish delighted in sending him out about three quarters of the way into a workout, and Rocky delighted in barking his head off as he slalomed among the runners as they sprinted around the track. Everyone thought this was just charming except the guys who were trying to hit their times, hold their form, and avoid the darting dog. Cam was particularly "vexed," to borrow his expression. He had a deathly fear of dogs, having been bitten by a pit bull when he lived in Jamaica, and as a result he had a serious blood feud working against the whole canine population.

After half-an-hour of dog dodging he turned and screeched, "Frankie, mi tink you a go talk to di mon 'bout him fool-ish-ness."

"I will. I haven't had a chance, yet."

"Mon you betta hurry; mi can't hava bumbaclot dog a run me down like a run-a-way slave. At a no fun dis, no sah."

"Maybe this is his idea of fun."

"Who? Fish a da dawg? Well a no fi mi. Let 'im come and run, and wi will tah up shout, 'Sic 'em, Rock.' Den wi see a who a hav fun."

"But what can we do it about it?" Russell frowned.

"Dawgie kin git sick, sumtimes," Cam said devilishly. "If da Rock no feel so good em na chasin' us sa fast."

"You wouldn't," I said.

"Ah would," said Cam. "Ya kno Stephane, dat youth en da French class?"

"Steve Pierre-Louis – that Haitian guy?"

"Yamon."

"What about him?"

"Dem say dat him mutha wok obya. Ya know – makin' duppy dahlly."

"Duppy dolly? What the hell is that?"

"Ya kna - dat voodoo shit, makin' dahls an such."

"You wouldn't do that to Rocky."

"If him keep run mi down mi would. All ah need's a bit a 'is 'air; Stephane's mutha do da res."

"That's cold; Rocky's a good dog."

"Bad tings 'a happen to good dawgs."

"I'm with Cam," said Russell. "Whatever he means."

Chapter 12

As Fish charged into the house after practice on Monday, he realized that he was in trouble before he fully opened the door. Not only was he an hour late for dinner, but he had forgotten that Maria's Spring Concert was scheduled for seven o'clock in the high school auditorium.

Everyone was already gone, and there was a note, written in fluent sarcasm, pinned to the kitchen counter by a half-filled water glass.

"You probably forgot about the concert – again - so we had to leave without you. Your ticket is on the dining room table. If it's not too much trouble, try to get there for some of it! – N."

Fish grabbed the ticket, dashed out the door, and hopped in his car – a rusted out 1990 Toyota with close to 200,000 miles on it. Affectionately dubbed "The Trackmobile" by generations of Westfield runners, the Corolla was a reliable old friend whose "get up and go" had "got up and gone." By the time Fish got to the school, it was intermission and the band had already finished its set.

"Did I miss much?" Fish whispered as he slid into his seat.

"Only the whole performance," his wife hissed.

"I'm sorry; something came up."

"Something always does."

"Does Maria know I wasn't here?"

"I don't know. Luckily, they can't see much from the stage with those spotlights in their eyes. When you weren't home by six-thirty, she gave up hope. You know, this is the third thing you've missed in the last two weeks."

"No it's not."

"Yes it is. You missed Matty's basketball game last week, after you promised him you'd be there, and you were late for Parent-Teacher Night; you got there in the sixth period."

"Late doesn't count as a miss."

"It does in my book, buddy."

"Now, we have to sit through the regular chorus, the select chorus, and every other goddamn chorus they can possibly think up," Fish muttered.

"Wages of sin," his wife said rather uncharitably.

"We'll go out for ice cream afterwards," Fish offered.

"Oh goody!" Nina replied. "That'll make everything just perfect."

Chapter 13

The next day, Fish noticed Nina acting more than usually pissed and didn't have to ask why. His latest apology was just one more meaningless mea culpa in an unending line, and while his wife had the patience of a saint, even the saints had their limits. Besides, three decades was a little long to put up with this stuff.

As for Fish, he felt like he was on a merry-go-round that wouldn't stop spinning. Splitting time three or four different ways was tough, and it was only getting tougher. Teaching was hard enough, but having the AP class and being the department chair added to his load. And coaching, even with three very capable assistants, took an enormous amount of time and energy. With his mother living alone and showing definite signs of age, he found himself constantly driving across town to fix things, bring things, or just see to things. That was just one more item on his already overflowing plate. And, there was also the matter of his own family – a wife and three children who, while very capable on their own, still needed him to be there. Everybody wanted a piece of Fish and there wasn't enough to go around. He barely slept at night and did nothing for himself, but somehow there was never enough time.

So, he continued to careen around town, racing from school to practice to his mom's to home. It wasn't the most relaxing lifestyle or the healthiest, but it was his and he was stuck with it for now.

Chapter 14

Shot put practice ran late today, mostly because Oscar couldn't stay in the circle. Now that he had learned to put the twelve-pound iron ball from his shoulder instead of chucking it like a baseball, the coaches were trying to keep him in the seven-foot throwing ring. But, it was like trying to keep a very clumsy bull in a really tiny china shop. If a thrower steps out of the circle before completing his throw it's a foul. Needless to say, Oscar's 330-plus pounds found the circle a tad confining.

"You gotta stay in O," Pell begged. "Otherwise it doesn't count."
Fish was standing on the side watching.
"I can't; the circle's too small."

"They're not gonna make it bigger just for you," Pell teased. "You've got to reverse. Switch your feet at the end. Then you can catch your right foot inside the toeboard."

Oscar looked perplexed.

"Here, watch me," Pell instructed.

Pell settled into the back of the circle with the shot in his right hand. He cradled it gently against the right side of his neck, and extended his left arm for balance. Leaning forward, he paused for a second, gathered himself, and suddenly slid backwards, turning and lifting in one smooth motion. The shot exploded out of his hand and flew high into the air before coming to rest more than fifty feet away.

"See, it's easy," Pell said. "Just take it one step at a time."

"It's easy for you," Oscar replied. "I can't do it."

"Yeah, you can," Pell argued. "Stop talkin' yourself out of it."

Oscar tried, but there was simply no way. Once his great bulk got moving, the laws of physics took hold. On his next attempt, he fouled again. On the one after that, he tripped over the toeboard. On his third try, he tangled his right foot under him and fell out of the ring, landing heavily on his right side ten feet into the throwing area. With both body and ego bruised, Oscar slowly climbed back to his feet.

"I suck!" he yelled.

"No you don't," Pell reassured him. "You're actually throwin' better; you're close to forty feet now. Once you learn how to stay in, you'll be fine."

"But I can't stay in."

"You will; you're gettin' closer."

Oscar didn't look much happier; he wasn't convinced. "Can I go home now?" he pleaded.

"Sure," Pell answered surprisingly. "We're about done for the day, right Fish?"

"Absolutely," Fish agreed. "C'mon Oscar, I'll give you a lift."

It was starting to rain and Oscar lived all the way on the other side of the parkway in a ragged little neighborhood called Spanish Town, but Fish didn't care; he had an ulterior motive for driving. They climbed into the Trackmobile, with Oscar overflowing the passenger seat, and headed off.

Following Oscar's directions, Fish guided the decrepit auto through the narrow streets, turning left at an abandoned gas station, right at the boarded-up community center, and left again at a tiny bodega. They pulled up in front of a shabby little cape in desperate need of a paint job and some serious TLC. The screen door was hanging precariously at a strange angle, and two of the upstairs windows were broken.

"Is anybody home?" Fish asked. "Maybe I could meet your parents, tell 'em how well you're doing."

"Probably not," Oscar replied.

"It's 6:30; when do you eat supper?"

"Whenever. My mom works late; we don't all eat at the same time."

"Who does the cooking? Not you, I hope."

"My sister, sometimes. Mostly, I just get something from the store or McDonald's."

"I see," Fish paused. He was starting to understand why Oscar weighed what he did. "What does your mother do?"

"She works."

"Where?"

"All over"

"All over?"

"Yeah, for other people…in their houses"

"Like a maid?"

"Yeah, like a maid, you know."

Oscar wasn't too talkative to begin with and this particular conversation was beginning to touch a nerve.

"How about your dad?" Fish persisted.

"I don't have one."

"Sure you do. Is he back in Mexico?"

"I said I don't have one." Oscar was getting angry now.

"OK. Take it easy. I'm just tryin', to help you out here."

"I don't need any help. I can take care of myself."

"All right, relax kid. It's gonna be all right."

"No it's not; it's not gonna be all right," Oscar yelled as he bolted from the car. He slammed the car door shut and quickly disappeared into the sorry little house.

Chapter 15

Avi Glick was a mess. A loner, though not by choice, he was tall, skinny, timid, and weak. He also had glasses, braces, a stutter, and an obsessive-compulsive disorder. Born the youngest of five children into a middle-class Jewish family, Avi was the forgotten child. While his brothers became doctors and his sisters became teachers, Avi became lost. To his accountant father, Marvin, Avi was a disappointment. To his seamstress mother, Ruthie, he was a baby. Dad yelled, mom protected, and Avi suffered in silence.

And, things weren't going any better at school. Ignored by most and tortured by some, whenever possible Avi retreated into his own little land of make believe. On all of his free periods and during lunch, he would find a secluded corner of the school's library and immerse himself in his secret passion – reading science fiction. There, he met his closest friends – Guy Montag, Billy Pilgrim, and the Starship Troopers. They didn't tease him and they certainly didn't judge. They were used to oddballs like Avi and they accepted him, no questions asked.

One curious thing about Avi, though, had been evident right from the start; he could run like a deer. And, he never got tired. In fact, he hardly even sweated. Although he had no muscle, he also had no fat. A salesman at the local Foot Locker had once measured Avi's body fat when he was buying running shoes, and the entire staff had been astonished at the reading of just over three percent. That was an Olympic athlete's level.

Avi had always been fast, even when he was a little kid. His father joked that he got so much practice running away from bullies that he had to be fast, and that was at least partially true, but the truth hurt. The thing was, Avi loved to run – but he didn't like to race. And, he especially didn't like to win. He didn't feel comfortable being way out in front; too much was expected and too many were watching. It was much easier being part of the crowd, so he would hang back in races, running alongside kids that he could easily blow away, just enjoying the gentle patter of his feet brushing lightly against the ground. Avi was a glider, one of those natural runners who moved effortlessly, not so much running as floating. And, while his body floated, so did his mind. Running was his escape, and it was only when his teammates and coaches yelled at him that he was jolted out of his reverie. To placate them, he would speed up and pass some runners - but never all of them. He would never win, even though he always could, because he didn't want to. He didn't feel like he deserved to.

Chapter 16

Another rainy Saturday practice beckoned, and with Opening Day only two days away the team wasn't even remotely close to being ready. With the Franklin North meet looming, the coaches had backed off on the training a bit – but just a tiny bit. They weren't getting soft; they just didn't want everyone exhausted for Monday.

Unfortunately for all concerned, Rocky was at practice again. He was his usual excited self, jumping and nipping at the runners' heels as they circled the track, but this time Cam had come loaded for…um…dog. Reaching into his green and yellow track bag with the Jamaican flag on it, he pulled out a chunk of what looked like black wool that had been crudely fashioned into the shape of a dog.

"What the fuck is that?" Frankie politely inquired.

"Dat's fi da Rock," Cam replied evenly. "Stephane's madda mek it. She said ees fooul-prooof."

"It'll have to be if you're gonna' use it."

"What are you gonna' do with it?" Russell asked. "Feed it to him?"

"Bumbaclot! Ya nah feed him it; ya stick it wid wah pin."

"What's that gonna' do?" Russ persisted. "It's just a piece of wool."

"A no wool, ya fool; dis a dally – wid a piece a di dawg 'air inside," Cam answered irritably. "Mi grabbed summa him 'air when ah wuz pettin' 'im. If da Rock doan feel so nice, you'll ah know da reason why."

Cam took a two-inch long hatpin out of his bag and stuck it into Voodoo Rocky's back right paw, but nothing happened.

"See," Russell said. "It's stupid."

"Jus' ya waita bit," Cam replied. "Lemme try a-gain."

This time he tried the back left paw, but still nothing. The dog continued to bounce around; by now he was chasing the distance guys as they ran their warm-up laps.

"This is dumb," Frankie said. "Let's get started."

"Wan more time," Cam muttered as he tried the right front paw.

Bingo! In an instant Rocky was on the ground whimpering and biting at his foot. Fish ran over and examined him.

"Let me see it boy; let me see your paw. Geez," he exclaimed, "How the hell did that happen?"

He called for one of the freshmen to bring him the med kit, and he grabbed the tweezers that we kept in there for taking out splinters and things. Reaching over to Rocky, he took the dog's paw and gently removed a half-inch thorn that had somehow become lodged there. Taking the peroxide out, Fish cleaned the wound and covered it with a Band-Aid, pre-wrap, and then some athletic tape. Rocky limped away, but he didn't seem to be any the worse for wear. However, everyone noticed that he lay quietly under a tree for the rest of practice.

Fish turned to Olson and said, "How the hell did he get a thorn in his foot, anyway? There aren't any rose bushes or anything out here."

Olson just shrugged his shoulders.

Cam smiled and said, "Ya see whey mi mean? Ya dun fuck wid Stephane's madda."

The team ran about half of a normal workout and spent the last thirty minutes on starts, sticks, and meet strategy. Since many of the guys had never been in a real track meet, there was plenty to go over. Fish started off by talking about the rules.

"There are alot of crazy rules in track and field, and most of them don't make much sense, but you still have to follow them," he began. "For example, you can't wear any jewelry, so those of you with earrings, necklaces, or bracelets, they have to come off."

Cam interrupted, "How come in da 'lympics ah see mah bwoy Usain wearin' 'is bling?"

"Because it's the Olympics, and they use international rules. We compete under state rules."

"Dat no fair. Wan sport – wan rule," Cam persisted.

"I'll tell you what. You run as fast as Usain Bolt, I'll let you wear your stuff. Watches are included; so those come off too. Uniforms are another thing. They're supposed to be identical."

That was going to be a challenge. With more than fifty guys on the team, there were no more than twenty uniforms that looked alike. All those tight-money budgets had forced the school to scrimp on uniforms, buying only a few a year to fill in for the ones that had gone missing. While all of them were in Westfield's familiar Kelly green, there were a ton of variations. Some had white lettering and trim and some had yellow. Some had Westfield in block letters and some in script. And, some just had Wildcats written across the front. It was a mess.

"In individual events, we can get away with slightly different uniforms," Fish continued, "but in the relays they have to be identical. So, some of you guys might have to swap tops."

"I nah wear Os-car's top, I promise ya dat," Cam whispered. "Dat bwoy sweats like a peeg."

"How can you wear Oscar's?" Frankie asked. "He's twice your size."

"Ee don't matta; ah would even wear Avi's 'fore dat."

"He's half your size; and I think he's got eczema."

"Wha name eggs-a-mah?"

"It's some kind of a skin disease."

"Den ah nah wear dat wan eda. Mi share wid ya."

"Except we run on the same relay."

Cam looked puzzled, but only for a second. Then his face brightened.

"Ya run da leadoff and ah'll run da anka. Den we kin change in da middle."

That would be a little strange, but at least Cam was thinkin'.

Fish had one more admonition.

"Oh yeah, watch your language, too; there's a no cursing rule. They call it unsportsmanlike conduct and the penalty is ejection from the meet and suspension from the next one, so it's serious."

"What do they mean by cursing?" Jenkins asked.

"Anything you can't say in polite company - like in front of your parents."

"We can say anything in my house," Russ jumped in. "You should hear my father watchin' the Mets, after he's had a couple of brewskis."

"My parents curse, too," said Steve McDermott, "especially my mother."

"Mine, too," added Andy Simmons.

"Frankly, I don't give a damn," said a visibly annoyed Fish. This meeting was taking far too much time, and there was way too much left to cover.

"You can't say that; isn't 'damn' a curse?" somebody yelled.

"How bout 'goddamn?'" asked another.

"How about 'hell?'" asked a third.

By now, Fish was officially pissed off.

"I don't know, and I don't give a flying fuck!" he yelled. "Now THAT'S a curse!"

Chapter 17

Sunday morning at the Fischettis' meant church and bagels, in that order. Getting everyone up at nine-thirty, the latest time possible to have the troops washed, dressed, and present at St. Ann's for ten-thirty mass, was no simple trick.

Matty was easy; he was up by eight, playing on the computer and enjoying his usual Sunday morning cereal buffet. The others were tougher. Maria was a sleepyhead and A.J. stayed out too late. Since Fish waited up watching ESPN reruns until everyone was in, he was usually tired, too.

"Everybody up!" Fish boomed. "Time for church."

"I don't feel good," A.J. groused. "My head hurts."

"It's called a hangover," his father replied. "How many beers did you have last night?"

"None!"

"Plus what?"

"Plus none!"

Fish knew that his son rarely drank, but he hated missing a chance to bust his chops.

"Maria, let's go. You look beautiful enough; God doesn't care."

"Dad, I'm getting dressed."

"Please leave them alone," his wife pleaded. "They'll be ready."

"I hate walking in late; everyone stares at us."

"At least our family goes to church. I teach in a Catholic school and half of my students don't go."

"That's nuts," Fish opined. "Why send your kids to Catholic school if you don't go to church? What's the point?"

"The point is that their parents don't want them in public school. Half of your district goes to religious schools."

She was right on that score. All of the Orthodox Jews that had moved into the community and attended private yeshivas had slashed the enrollment at Westfield, robbing the school of many of its top students.

"Who's saying mass today?" A.J. grunted as he dashed for the car.

"Father Adibi usually says the ten-thirty," his mother replied.

"He's sooo boring; I can't understand anything he says," Maria complained.

"I like him," Matty chimed in. "He's funny."

"You like him because he's fast," his brother responded.

Fish had to agree. The parish's new Nigerian priest seemed like a good guy, but he was completely unintelligible because of his thick accent and hopelessly fractured English. No matter how hard Fish tried to concentrate on the homily, he soon found himself drifting off, thinking about school, track, and a million other things before being jolted back by the jingling of the collection plate or the voices of the chorus.

"It'll be fine," Fish concluded. "The mass will be fast. And, then it's bagel time."

"And that's how we teach the children the true meaning of religion," his wife needled.

Chapter 18

Today was opening day, and Fish was suffering from his usual pre-meet butterflies. He'd been really nervous all day, probably because he knew that his team wasn't ready, even cutting short his lesson in eighth period American Lit so that the kids could start their homework early and he could fine tune his meet plan.

The squad piled into two buses for the short ride to Franklin North, Fish and Cahill on the first bus, and Pell and Olson on the second. The guys who were in the early events, the hurdlers, milers, long jumpers, and shot putters, always rode the first bus. That way, the second bus could wait for stragglers or load extra equipment and not deliver guys too late for their warm-ups.

It was a cold, raw day, but at least it wasn't raining. Early season meets in the northeast are the worst. The temperature drops, the wind howls, and it's usually wet. There's no way anyone can hit a time or distance, so everyone just tries his best, takes whatever points possible, and hopes to get out of there without getting hurt. Today would be no exception.

Today's opponents, the Franklin North Falcons, were an up and coming team. Energized by their hot-shot young coach, and sporting brand-new, crimson uniforms to match their recently resurfaced track, the Falcons radiated confidence. They saw Westfield as an over-the-hill squad whose best years, much like Fish's, were squarely in the rear view mirror. For today, at least, they were right.

In dual meets, a team gets five points for first place, three for second, and one for third. Relays, because there are only two teams running, count five - zip. So, after "Little Frankie" won the opening event, the intermediate hurdles, and Franklin North took second and third, Westfield led by one point. That turned out to be their only lead of the day.

The Falcons swept the 100, which was highlighted by Demond Green's running out of his lane. Greenie's act had been seen before, but it never failed to amaze. The 100 is run on a straightaway - there's no way to go out of your lane unless you're cross-eyed or drunk - but Demond still managed to do it on a semi-regular basis.

When Fish asked him how this could possibly have happened again, Greenie hung his head and mumbled, "I don't know; there's too many lines out there."

"Jesus Christ, Greenie, you've run the 100 a million times," Fish said morosely. "All you have to do is go straight."

Demond didn't say anything; he just slumped his shoulders and looked sad.

Fish shook his head and walked away.

"I ought to put fuckin' blinders on him, like a horse," he muttered to no one in particular.

North Franklin then took one and two in the mile when Avi suddenly stopped trying on the third lap. He had been looking great, running effortlessly with the leaders, when he suddenly throttled back to jog with the slowpokes. After the event, as usual, he had no rational explanation for his actions, and Fish and Cahill both glared daggers at him. Cam won the 400 easily, but Franklin again took second and third. When they swept the 800, with three kids running well ahead of the field, the rout was on. They dominated the field events, traditionally a Westfield strength, as the jumpers accomplished nothing and Oscar, in his first real competition, produced six consecutive fouls, three in the shot and three more in the disc. By the time the relays rolled around, Franklin was up by forty and Fish had all the freshmen and sophomores on the track.

Strangely enough, there wasn't much yelling on the bus ride home. Fish and Cahill huddled in the front two seats going over times and numbers, but there wasn't much to learn. Franklin was the better team, plain and simple, and unless something changed dramatically it promised to be a very long season for the Wildcats.

Chapter 19

While Fish hadn't yelled much yesterday, he'd obviously been saving it up for today. As soon as attendance was taken and the team had started to stretch, he let them have it.

"Gentlemen," (a salutation that always promised trouble) he began, "that was one piss-poor showing yesterday. There are exactly 141 points available in a dual track meet. Does anyone know how many we scored?"

When no one piped up, Fish answered the question for himself.

"Forty-five! That's how many we scored! Carbone, you're a little math whiz; how many does that leave for North Franklin?"

"Uh, I'm not much of a math whiz, coach," Frankie confessed.
Andrew Chang, a pint-sized two-miler, was the team's resident math geek.

"You can sure as hell subtract, though, can't you?" Fish continued.

"Yeah"

'So what's the answer?"

"Uh, ninety-six?"

"That's right! That's goddamn right! Ninety-six!" Fish said, as he turned his attention back to the team. "That means they beat us better than two to one. Out of seventeen events, we won a grand freakin' total of four. Frankie won both hurdles, and Cam won the 200 and the quarter. That's it! We lost all three relays, too. The rest of our points were in garbage time when they weren't even trying anymore. That is some sad shit, and you should all be ashamed of yourselves; I know I am. That was NOT Westfield Track!" Fish was screaming now. "And, that is NOT who we are. If you guys thought practice was tough before, you ain't seen nothin' yet. Break up into your groups and get started – we've got plenty of work to do."

Chapter 20

After practice, Oscar walked home. It was close to two miles, but he didn't care. He had half a sandwich left over from lunch for the first part of the trip, and he could stop at the convenience store to pick up something for the last stretch. He always got plenty to eat at school because the lunch ladies loved him. They were all locals who looked out for their own and they loaded up his plate, teasing that he'd better finish it all. Oscar didn't like to disappoint them. Thus fortified, he could usually make it through practice without snacking and incurring the wrath of the coaches. But, on the journey home all bets were off.

Nearing his house, Oscar went into the seven-eleven on Jefferson Street and bought two hot pockets and a Dr. Pepper. He ate one sandwich before he got to the corner and finished the other one a block later. Then he washed them down with the soda. As soon as he rounded the corner to his house, he spotted the battered, black Ford pick-up parked about three feet from the curb. The bumper sticker that read, "My Other Ride Is Your Girlfriend," was the giveaway. Nando, his mother's latest boyfriend, was around, and that always meant trouble.

Oscar pushed the front door gently. It was never locked and it opened easily. Peering in to the small living room, he saw that it was empty. Discarded fast food containers were scattered around and the curtain on the cracked back window flapped in the early evening breeze.

"Carmen?" he called.

But his sister didn't answer. That was weird. It was six-forty and no one was home. Someone should've been around and something should've been on the stove. He went into the tiny bedroom that his sister and mother shared – but still no one. Calling again, Oscar searched the kitchen and bathroom - nothing. Where was everyone?

He went back outside and looked around. The sky was darkening now and the street was deserted. He sat down on the front steps and decided to wait.

Chapter 21

The next morning was bright and sunny with only a few wispy clouds in the sky, but Oscar never made it to school. Nobody was around to make him go, and he was still worried about his mother and sister. He didn't know where anybody was, and Nando's pick-up was still parked out front.

He spent most of the morning watching cartoons and playing video games. There wasn't much to eat in the house, so he grabbed some loose change from the salsa jar his mother kept on the kitchen table and headed down to the raggedy Old El Paso bodega on the corner. He picked up a breakfast burrito and some juice there, and then returned home to lounge on the couch and watch reruns of *Teenage Mutant Ninja Turtles* until the front door pushed open.

The missing threesome sauntered in without a care in the world.

"Where were you?" Oscar whined. "I was up all night waitin' for you, ma."

His mother looked tired, hung over, or both.

"Don' worry baby," she slurred. "Is all good. Nando took us to the city; we was dancin', partyin', havin' a good time. You know."

Oscar didn't know.

"You coulda called," he added.

"I tried baby, but my phone was dead."

Nando shot Oscar a wicked grin.

"We was busy, ya know what I mean? What was you worried 'bout anyway Fatboy - missin' a meal?"

Oscar glared back at him. Nando was a showoff and a bully, and he had a reputation on the streets – a bad one. He always had cash in his pockets and he liked to flash it around, but exactly how he came by it was a mystery. He usually had one scam or another going and there were rumors that he sold drugs out of the back of his truck. He did have money, though, and to a struggling single mother that was an attractive trait.

"Here baby, we got some lefovers from the party," his mother said. "You want some?"

Oscar wasn't hungry. Every time his mother messed up she tried to fix it with food. And since she messed up quite often, he was always eating.

"I don't want no food ma; I want you around."

"Yo, she a grown woman Homes," Nando cut in. "She can go where she wants. Know what I'm sayin'?"

"Shut up, Nando!" Oscar yelled. "It's none of your business."

"Yeah, is my business. Now that I'm wit yo mama, everythin's my business."

Carmen had retreated to the safety of the back bedroom and mama wasn't talking, so it was all on Oscar now. His mother watched silently as the two men in her life squared off.

"We don't need you Nando; we don't even want you here."

"I think you do, big boy. I know yo mama does. Ain't that right, Mija?"

Mija made no reply.

"Tell him to get out, Ma. We don't need his dirty money."

There was no response.

"Get out, Nando! Get the hell out! Now!" Oscar screamed at the top of his lungs.

"Why don' you make me, Fatboy?"

"Maybe I will."

Nando stood defiantly in the middle of the room. With his arms folded nonchalantly in front of his chest, he waited calmly for Oscar to make his move. Nando was tall, but not as tall as Oscar and nowhere near as heavy. He was quick and strong, though, and the scars on his face and hands, some old and some very new, were proof that he'd been in more than his share of scraps.

Oscar stood frozen, unsure of what to do. He had made the mistake of challenging Nando, and now there was no way out.

"Whatcha waitin' for Gordito?" Nando sneered, using Oscar's mother's pet name for him. "I thought you was gonna do somethin'."

His mother giggled nervously, but Oscar snapped. Dropping his head, he rushed at Nando like a wild bull, but the wiry street fighter easily sidestepped him and then kicked Oscar in the ass as he stumbled by.

"Hey, it's a boool fight," Nando jeered. "C'mon Toro, Toro, come to papa."

Gritting his teeth, Oscar charged again. This time Nando didn't move at all. His heavy boot shot up and caught Oscar square in the stomach. Oscar fell to the floor and started to retch.

"Hey, don' mess up the floor, Toro. Wait 'til you get back in the barn."

"That's enough, Nando," Oscar's mother yelled. "Leave him alone."

"He wans to be a man, let him act like a man. Gettin' his ass kicked be good for him."

Oscar tried one last time. Driving up off the floor with all his strength, he lunged at his tormenter but missed again. This time Nando cuffed him on the ear and shoved him across the room. Then he opened the front door wide.

"Why don' YOU get out?" Nando taunted. "Come back when you a man."

Oscar looked at his mother, but her head was in her hands and she was sobbing softly.

The big boy gathered what little remained of his dignity, clambered to his feet slowly, and walked out the front door. He didn't look back.

Chapter 22

When Oscar finally showed up at school the next day he looked even scruffier than usual. His thick black hair was all matted, he still had on yesterday's clothes, and he was limping a little. Frankie caught up to him just before first period as he was coming out of the cafeteria. Oscar's tray was loaded with a stack of silver dollar-sized pancakes, a bunch of those little breakfast sausages, and a couple of containers of milk, but he was still walking a little unsteadily.

"What up O?" Frankie greeted him. "Looks like somebody had a rough night. Didn't hurt your appetite, though."

Oscar mumbled something back that was inaudible.

"For real, what happened dude? You look like shit."

"Nothin'. Nothin' happened."

"Man, I'd love to play poker with you 'cause you're one lousy liar. Somethin's up."

"Nothin's up. I don't wanna talk about it anyway."

"I hear you bro, but you gotta talk to somebody. How 'bout the Fishman?"

"No!"

"Why not?"

"Cause he'd just make some stupid joke and laugh."

"How 'bout Pell, then? He wouldn't laugh."

"I dunno, maybe. Maybe later. I'll see."

Frankie went on his way, but later in the day Oscar did stop by the gym where he caught Pell at the end of sixth period. After he opened up about the whole story, from the time he got home right up until the fight with Nando and walking out the door, Pell reacted…like…well…Pell.

"Where is this punk?" Pell roared. "I'll kick his fuckin' ass."

That was Pell's other default position on solving life's little problems.

"What's his name?" he raged. "Nacho? Where's this asshole hang out?"

"Nah, nah," Oscar tried hard not to laugh. "No, not Nacho…it's Nando, and he's my mother's boyfriend; that won't work."

"Yeah it will; he beat you up. That's bullshit! He's a grown man fighting a kid. That's worse than bullshit, that's some cowardly shit – cowardly bullshit!"

Pell was still pissed, but he looked a little calmer now that he'd put a proper label on Nando's behavior.

"He didn't really beat me up; he coulda done alot worse. He just pushed me around a little. I started it all, anyway."

"Doesn't matter. He shoulda backed off; you're just a kid."

Pell was right on that score.

"I just need a place to stay for right now," Oscar said. "I can't go back home."

Pell looked pensive for a minute.

"You got any relatives around?"

"I got an aunt, but she's got three little kids, and I got a cousin who lives in the city, but that's too far."

"Any friends? Anybody who can take you in?"

"Nah, nobody's got any room. All my friends have brothers and sisters and nieces and nephews stayin' with 'em. There's nobody."

Pell paused again. Who could take this kid for a while?

"Tell you what, let me talk to Fish about this. He knows alot of people."

"I kinda didn't want him to know."

"Why not?"

"I dunno. He'd probably think it's funny or somethin'."

"No he wouldn't, and he might have an idea. Let me see what he thinks."

Not surprisingly, when Pell talked to Fish later that afternoon the head coach did have an idea. His plan was to have Pell, a confirmed bachelor who lived alone, take Oscar in. The ensuing conversation did not go well.

"No way! No fuckin' way!" Pell protested. "I can't have Oscar livin' with me. Call Social Services; they'll find a place for him."

"Yeah, but probably not in our district." Fish responded. "That would undo everything we're trying to accomplish."

"I can't take him – no way."

"Why not? Give me one good reason."

"I'll give you three. First off, it's illegal. Second, I don't have the room. And third, people will think I'm a perv, a single guy havin' an eighteen-year-old boy livin' in his apartment with him."

"It's only gonna be for a little while, and he's eighteen; so that makes it legal," Fish countered. "And, you do have the room, and people already think you're a pervert. This'll just confirm it."

Pell didn't laugh, and Fish wasn't done.

"C'mon, he's being abused at home. You can keep an eye on what he eats, too."

"He doesn't look abused."

"But he is. His mother's never there, and when she is this other clown's always around. We should probably do something for his sister, too."

"Want me to take her in, too?" Pell asked sarcastically.

"Nah, not yet," Fish grinned. "How about that little room in the back, the one you euphemistically call an office? You could stick Oscar in there."

Pell pondered the sanctity of his three-room apartment. "I got all my football stuff in there - videos, playbooks, all kinds of shit. How about givin' him to Kev or Josh?"

He knew the answer to that question before he asked it. Coach Cahill had a wife, four kids, and a modest little ranch house that wasn't even in the district. Coach Olson had a one-bedroom apartment and a gorgeous live-in girlfriend; having Oscar around would definitely cramp his style.

"I don't think so," Fish replied. "It's you or the streets."

"Why don't you take him? You've got a big house. Shit, you've got four bedrooms and a basement."

"And a wife, three kids, a dog, and a mortgage. You da man, Pell!"

"Shit! Shit! Shit!"

"Then you'll do it?'

"Shit! Shit! Shit!"

"I'll take that as a yes," Fish concluded.

Chapter 23

Practice the last two days was harder than ever. The weather had warmed up a little which helped, but not too much. Determined to whip the team into shape, even if it killed them, the coaches were unrelenting. Usually, they followed a training pattern called the "Bowerman Method," named after some old guy who coached at Oregon about a hundred years ago. Basically, it means that you train hard one day and go easy the next so your body can recover. Anything that carries the "Oregon Stamp of Approval" is considered gospel by track coaches since Eugene, Oregon, and the University of Oregon located there, is the Mecca of American distance running. And, Fish usually followed that model. But now things had changed. There was a hard workout on Wednesday, a harder one on Thursday, and even today, with the season's first invitational coming up tomorrow, the boys ran hard. It was a discouraged and beaten bunch of runners that trudged off the track at the end of practice.

"Bus leaves at eight-thirty sharp tomorrow, back of the high school," Fish yelled. "Don't be late. If you miss the bus, it's five penalty miles before you can compete. And, we have a meet on Monday against Brookside. So, be on time."

Chapter 24

At eight-twenty the next morning, on a chilly April the first, the bus was only half full. The coaches looked around anxiously, but the seats weren't filling up.

"What the hell's this, an April Fool's joke?" Fish groused. "Another ten minutes, Nicky," he said to the team's long-time bus driver.

Nicky DeRosa, a former Westfield football player, had been driving the track bus for as long as anyone could remember. The guys all loved him because he was Westfield through and through and he understood athletes. He knew that after a long Saturday meet all the guys wanted on the ride home was to listen to their music and eat, so he let them. He didn't yell if somebody put his feet on the seat across from him or if a couple of food wrappers ended up on the floor. He also knew every shortcut known to man, which sure came in handy when they were rushing to a meet. Unlike other sporting events, track meets don't wait for all the competitors to arrive; if a team isn't there on time, the meet starts without them.

Ten minutes later some guys were still missing, nine to be exact, so it definitely wasn't a prank. Fish waited a minute or two more, and then gave Nicky the sign to pull out. The team headed to the meet, about twenty minutes away and jauntily titled the Jamestown Jamboree, decidedly shorthanded. Among the more notable absentees were the second and third distance guys, Andy Simmons and Steve McDermott, the number one vaulter, Mike Howley, and Oscar, who had talked his way onto his aunt's couch for a few days until Pell could prepare for his arrival. The other MIA's were freshmen and sophomores who were new to the team and didn't fully grasp the gravity of their mistake.

Missing a track meet was the one unpardonable sin at Westfield. If a guy missed a practice and had a good excuse, the coaches might let him slide. If he missed a practice and didn't have a good excuse, he'd have to run extra the next day. But since the penalty was usually just a mile or two, it was no big deal. Missing a meet, however, was a very big deal. The first time it happened the penalty was a timed five-mile run. The second infraction cost ten miles. There was no third time – the season was over. That was the one immutable and ironclad rule of Westfield Track.

With nine guys missing today, Tuesday's practice promised to be a bloodbath. Some of these guys couldn't even run five miles, let alone hit a time. And, what would Oscar do? He couldn't make it home from school without snack breaks. Plus, the missing guys wouldn't be allowed to compete Monday against a team that was quite beatable. This was definitely going to be a problem.

The Jamboree turned out to be something less than advertised. With only eight teams attending, none of them powerhouses, Westfield should've done alot better than they did. Medals were awarded to the first six places in every event, but the Wildcats only went home with a total of five. Frankie finished third in the highs and fourth in the intermediates, having trouble with both a strong headwind and his steps. Cam won the 200, running an easy twenty-three flat, and then took second in the quarter, his least favorite race. Other than that, only Steve Jacobson, a nutty left-handed pole vaulter who managed to grab a surprise bronze on fewer misses, managed an award. The bus arrived home around six o'clock, carrying a tired and hungry bunch of Wildcats who were very worried about what Monday would bring.

Chapter 25

What Monday brought was rain - all day long. When school started it was drizzling, at lunch it was pouring, and by three o'clock it had turned into a deluge. Although every school has a synthetic track now, meets still get rained out because the field events get dangerous. The good news was that the meet was postponed; the bad news was that practice wasn't.

Now, despite the rain and dankness, this was a good chance for the Saturday delinquents to make up their penalty miles, but not all of them recognized this great opportunity. As soon as the team finished stretching, Fish put "The Westfield Nine" on the starting line. All of them except Oscar had to complete the five-mile run, twenty laps of the track, in under forty-five minutes. Nine minutes a mile isn't very fast if you're in any kind of shape, but most of these guys had never run close to that distance in one shot. Since Oscar was a weight man, he got an hour to complete his run. The whistle blew and off they went into what Fish called, "the Night's Plutonian shore."

For Simmons and McDermott, who had both overslept, and for two little freshmen distance runners who had gotten to the high school five minutes after the bus left, the punishment was no problem. They breezed through, running eight-minute miles and chatting while they ran. For the others, though, it was no laughing matter. Mike Howley was a fine athlete, but the only way he ever traveled five miles was on his brand new, canary yellow Kawasaki Ninja. Not having any idea of how to pace himself, he ran the first mile in five-thirty and then had to walk two laps to recover. This rather bizarre strategy of alternately running and walking put him perilously close to the time limit, but he sprinted the last lap to raucous applause and finished with ten seconds to spare. Three others, all non-scoring types, dropped out.

And then there was Oscar, who when Fish asked why he had missed the bus simply dropped his little pinhead and shrugged his shoulders. Starting at what amounted to a brisk walk, he jogged a little, walked a little, ran a very little, and then walked some more. He only had to average twelve minutes a mile, but his first mile took thirteen and his second fourteen. He took a break between miles two and three, with the watch running, and then clocked sixteen minutes for mile three. When his hour was up, he still had more than four laps to go and Fish told him to stop, but Oscar ignored him and kept on truckin'. He was hardly moving by now, his massive chest heaving with every breath and his enormous legs taking tiny little pigeon steps like Babe Ruth trotting around the bases in one of those old baseball movies, but he kept on going even though there was no point to it.

The rain was still pelting down, his face had turned bright red, and he was sweating bullets. Fish looked worried as he turned to his assistants who were standing beside him.

"Pell, where's that defibrillator?" he asked.

"In the back hall."

"Better get it."

"You're kidding, right?"

"No...I'm not! Look at him. He looks like he's going to keel over any second."

"Why don't you just order him off the track?"

"I did, but he kept on going. Look at the kids, though; this is amazing."

It was amazing. The entire team had stopped what they were doing to watch the drama unfold. Ringing the track individually, in twos, and in threes, and positioned along the inside lane, the team began to cheer on their lumbering giant.

"OS-CAR!"

"OS-CAR!"

"OS-CAR!"

If Oscar heard them, he never let on. His face was a stone mask as the chant reverberated, softly at first, then louder and louder until everyone was yelling at the top of his lungs.

"OS-CAR!"

"OS-CAR!"

"OS-CAR!"

The girls team joined in next, their high-pitched voices topping the chorus, then the custodians and groundskeepers, half of them bellowing in Spanish, and finally even the coaches, with Pell's deep bass underscoring the din. Everyone was screaming, yelling like crazy, pumping their fists, and rooting the big boy home.

With the clock long shut off and the mob still chanting his name, Oscar sprinted the last ten yards, threw his hands into the air triumphantly, and collapsed in a heap onto the faded green track.

Chapter 26

That night at dinner, Fish was relating the story of Oscar's run to his family.

"It was the damndest thing. The kid wouldn't stop, no matter what. It was like Rocky. I thought he was gonna have a heart attack, for sure."

"Why didn't he stop?" his wife asked. "It sounds horrible."

"I don't know," Fish said. "But there's something about him. Frankie told me afterwards that the only thing Oscar would say when they got back to the locker room was, 'I'm no quitter - I'm a man.'"

"He didn't make the time, though, did he?"

"Are you kiddin'? Not even close."

"Are you going to make him run it again? You really can't do that, you know; it would be child abuse."

"I know. He really should run it, though; he barely finished. We shut the clock off on him when he had about a mile to go. And, all the kids who stopped running have to do it again. It wouldn't be fair."

"Fair? You said that he weighs 300 pounds and was about to have a stroke. How fair does it have to be?"

"He's more like three-forty, and he was red as a beet, but he still didn't get it done."

"Why don't you let him slide, dad?" A.J. jumped in. "You said he really tried. You always tell us that's the most important thing."

"I lied," Fish said staring stone-faced and straight ahead. He wasn't going to own up to that quote right now, but he had said it even if he didn't mean it. And, he certainly wasn't going to have his own words turned against him by his son, although he did recognize the logic in them.

"He did try. He tried harder than anybody I've ever seen," Fish admitted.

"Then let him stay," his wife said. "What's the problem?"

"The problem is the other guys. They didn't do it and they're suspended."

"The other guys don't weigh 300 pounds," Nina retorted.

"And they quit running, right?" Maria piped up. "At least Oscar finished."

"Barely"

"So, there's your rationale," his wife concluded. "He finished the run; now you can do what you want. You ARE the head coach."

"Don't remind me," Fish replied.

"OS-CAR!" Maria whispered, mimicking her dad's retelling of the story.

"OS-CAR!" Matty's squeaky voice joined in.

"OS-CAR!" A.J. yelled at the top of his lungs.

And then his wife joined in, her sweet soprano soaring above the others.

"OS-CAR!"
"OS-CAR!"
"OS-CAR!"

Fish knew when he was beaten.

"All right! All right! You all win!" he relented. "He can stay – Oscar can stay."

Chapter 27

Today was bright and sunny, with the temperature around sixty-five and a light breeze blowing down the backstretch. It was the first nice day in a while and a good omen for the afternoon make-up meet against the Brookside Fighting Badgers.

The meet was at home, so instead of riding the bus the team got to prepare the track. That meant setting up the hurdles, putting together the high jump and pole vault landing mats, raking out the long jump pit, and taking out the blocks, shots, and discs. When all that was done, the boys jogged a lap as a team and then broke into their event groups to get ready.

Success in track and field is based, at least somewhat, on preparation. It's not only about warming up and stretching; it's about getting ready for the actual events. Hurdlers spend half an hour doing drills before they run - lead legs, trail legs, five-step-in-betweens, and some starts to the first hurdle. Then they're ready to rock-n-roll. The jumpers and throwers have their own routines, too. Jumpers practice their steps over and over, trying to hit the exact same mark, at the exact same speed, every single time. In the horizontal jumps, taking off even a hair over the board results in a foul, and with only three attempts there's not much room for error. High jumpers and pole vaulters have an additional worry

– the fear factor. High jumpers almost all use the Fosbury Flop technique, which causes them to land on their backs or, more precisely, their shoulders and necks. The vaulters, who fall from much greater heights, often twelve or thirteen feet, have to hit their marks on the runway. Even a slight mistake at takeoff can put a vaulter in a dangerous place. It's the one really scary event in track and field, and guys have been paralyzed and even killed from vault landings gone wrong. Hanging upside down on a three-inch ribbon of fiberglass definitely attracts the crazies, and every team has a lunatic vaulter. Westfield was lucky enough to have three.

It could have been the weather, the opponent, the giddiness left over from Oscar's run, or a combination of all three, but the "Mildcats," as they were derisively called, almost got their first win. "Little Frankie" took both hurdles and led off the winning four by four, and Cam won the 200 and 400 before anchoring the same relay. The distance guys did all right too, mostly because Brookside stunk. Avi actually led the deuce until the final straightaway when he graciously allowed several people to pass him. Fortunately, two of them were his teammates. Still, weaknesses in the sprints and jumps proved fatal, and the Fighting Badgers prevailed by the score of 73-68. Fish wasn't into moral victories, and he probably figured that if he couldn't beat Brookside he'd never beat anybody, so he wasn't exactly beaming as he trudged dejectedly off the track.

Chapter 28

"So, are you feeling a little better now?" Pell inquired. "We almost won; maybe we don't suck so bad after all."

"Nah, we still lost," Fish answered. "And, we still suck. Brookside's awful and they beat us. What does that tell you? Saturday's the Sectional Relays; that'll give us a chance to look at a bunch of teams. We'll see what Kingsbridge and Greenmont have, not that it's gonna matter."

"We've got to make up some relay teams too," Cahill advised. "That whole meet's relays, even the field events."

"We can make up teams, lots of 'em, but they won't be any good. We don't exactly have a ton of quality depth," Fish grumbled.

Relay meets are fun because they're different. Track is really a series of individual events masquerading as a team sport. At the end of the meet they add up the points to find out who won. It's only in the relays that athletes really get to work together. This meet would feature field event relays, where three guys add their marks together to get a team score, as well as running events. In the running relays, four runners carry a baton (a twelve-inch aluminum tube that represents an old-time scroll) around the track. Not only do runners love relays, but fans do, too. Because they're the last events, the meet is often on the line when it's relay time. Traditionally, the mile relay, or 4 X 400 meters, is the closing event in a track meet. It's considered the classic relay race not only because of its long history, but because all four runners must have that hard-to-find combination of speed and endurance necessary to run a fast quarter.

Conversely, the sprint relay, or 4 X 100, requires great speed and precision passing but no endurance whatsoever. It's over in the blink of an eye. While those sprinters often leave the track disappointed, they're rarely in any pain. The 4 X 800, on the other hand, is for middle and distance runners. In high school, it's where coaches put slow guys who are in decent shape and can run two laps without passing out.

But the 4 x 4 is special. For one thing, it hurts. Three quarters of the way through the lap, lungs burning and legs turning to jelly, there's still another straightaway to run - the longest 100 meters ever. It takes strength, poise, and a whole lot of heart to finish strong. Westfield only had two guys who could run a decent 400 – Frankie and Cam. Frankie only liked it because there were no hurdles in his way, and Cam didn't like it at all. Nevertheless, Fish was bound and determined to enter a strong 4 X 4 team in Saturday's meet.

"On the line!" Fish roared at the beginning of practice. "Mile relay tryouts! Let's see who's got some balls besides Frankie and Cam."

The assistant coaches quickly herded anybody with a measurable pulse onto the track and assigned heats and lanes. When they were done, there were four heats of six runners each, with the first heat being the fastest. Frankie and Cam, with their spots on the relay assured, helped with the timing. All of the other sprinters and distance guys were involved, as well as a few jumpers and hurdlers. Only the shot putters and discus throwers were exempt from the proceedings.

Since it was practice and nobody was wearing spikes, the times were bound to be a little slow. Unfortunately, they turned out to be alot slow. In the first heat, The Notorious D.I.G. (Demond Isaiah Green) shot out to a huge lead. Running furiously, he veered all over the track visiting three different area codes. Halfway through he was up by twenty-five meters, but he was dead. The combination of his reckless style and the extra ground he was covering proved to be too much for him to handle. As he labored through the second curve, lactic acid seized his legs and turned them to cement. Coming down the stretch, his stride shortened to the point where he was almost walking. By the time he finally finished he had faded to fourth, and Russell Grimaldi, our sophomore quarter man, took the race in 57.5. Middle distance and distance guys populated the next two heats, but nobody broke a minute and Fish was getting testy.

"No wonder we stink!" Fish yelled. "Nobody can break fifty-seven. We need four guys, gentlemen, not two. Maybe we can have Frankie run two legs and Cam the other two; that might work!"

Fish's sarcasm wasn't lost on anyone, but contrary to his intentions it didn't make anybody run faster either. The spirit was willing but the flesh was way too weak - until the last heat anyway.

Running in a mixed group with two freshmen sprinters, two long jumpers, and Mike Howley, Avi Glick nervously pawed the starting line with his left foot. Subconsciously, he was already ticking off the reasons why he couldn't possibly run well: the race was too short, his favorite distance was the mile, he had never run a quarter before, and the other kids were all faster than him. By the time he had reached, "And, I have to pee," he was programmed to lose. Then Fish blew his whistle and off they went.

When Avi ran, the ugly duckling morphed into a beautiful swan. He moved fluidly, with no wasted motion, and his long strides ate up the ground. Since he was in so much better shape than the motley crew opposing him, he simply ran with them until they tired out. Then, suddenly finding himself twenty meters clear of the field with 100 to go, Avi panicked. Unwilling to finish first, he hit the brakes hard and slowed down until the second place runner came alongside. Then, he simply adjusted his speed slightly to match his teammate's pace. Striding in together, they passed the finish line almost simultaneously, with Avi pulling up just a bit to make sure he didn't cross first. The time was only 57.3, but between slowing down and refusing to pass his teammate, Avi had lost a good three or four seconds. We had another mile relay runner – he just didn't know it yet.

Chapter 29

Friday is the traditional test day in high schools, and Westfield is a traditional school. Teachers say that they give tests on Fridays because they want weekly summaries of what kids have learned, but it's really to give themselves a break after teaching a whole week. In any event, today was Friday.

Frankie had four tests on tap: a double physics test periods one and two, followed by a calculus test, an oral Spanish exam, and an Advanced Placement English test, in Fish's class, period eight. They had just finished reading Herman Melville's *Billy Budd* and now they had to write an essay on it.

Frankie knew the book well, and as near as he could figure Avi was alot like Billy Budd, right down to the debilitating stutter. According to Fish, Budd was "an innocent trapped in a hostile world where innocence cannot survive," and to Frankie that pretty much described Avi, although he was nowhere near as handsome as Budd. In the book, this evil guy named Claggart hated Budd for no good reason. That was kind of like the football players and the mean girls who picked on Avi because he wasn't "cool." Budd also knew this old guy, the Dansker, who gave him some cryptic advice he could never figure out. The advice was good, but Budd didn't believe it and he couldn't understand it anyway. That was like Fish and Avi. Fish always told Avi the right stuff, but Avi either couldn't make sense of it or couldn't put it into practice. At the end of the book, after Claggart had bugged him once too often, Budd went crazy and punched him out, killing him on the spot. Then, according to the Law of the Sea or something, Budd was hanged. It was hard to imagine Avi decking anybody, but he was definitely a candidate to crack up at any moment. In any event, the ending of the book sucked. It didn't seem fair that Budd had to die because Claggart was such a jerk, and Frankie didn't want to think what it all might mean for Avi.

Chapter 30

The bus took off at nine o'clock sharp on Saturday morning, rolling towards the Sectional Relays at Sutton Park. Much like Westfield High School, Sutton was also well past its prime. The bushes and grounds were seriously overgrown, the aluminum bleachers creaked in the wind, and the once spotless track was a pockmarked shell. When Sutton had hosted the State Games some years back, corporate sponsors had paid for the track to be totally redone. It had been resurfaced and relined, the pits had been replaced, and new windbreaks had been installed. But all of that was long gone. Now, the track was brick hard and faded to the point where on a cold day pin spikes wouldn't dig in at all, turning running into skating. The landing pits were old and torn, with pieces of foam peeking through the rips, and the takeoff boards for the jumps were cracked and broken. The circles in the weight events were only barely visible, and worst of all were their old-time "Hurdles of Death" – big, clunky things that weighed about fifty pounds each. When somebody hit one it was like hitting a stone wall; the hurdle didn't go down – the hurdler did. Because today's meet wasn't for points, the pressure was off. The goal was to try to win some medals, and it'd be a chance for the coaches to fool around with the relays.

The shuttle hurdles were up first and they didn't go well at all. In this race, four hurdlers from each team race back and fourth, side-by-side, with no baton passing. Teams need four good guys to do anything and Westfield only had one and a half. Fish had Frankie lead off because he knew what was going to happen on the last two legs. Carbone's sixteen flat into the wind was fine and put the team into the lead, but the number two guy, an Indian kid named Kavi Patel who was just learning to hurdle, ran seventeen and change coming back. At that point the team was in third place and still looking all right, but their third hurdler had to four-step all the way and the anchorman five-strided. Needless to say, there weren't any medals waiting at the finish line. It also set a sorry tone for the rest of the day.

The jumpers were fouling, the throwers were tumbling out of the circles, the sprinters were screwing up sticks, and the distance guys were running like snails. Two runners missed their races, and little Danny Kerrigan, a freshman distance guy who could barely run at all, managed to do something unique. Running the third leg on some sad little Frosh-Soph Relay team, he waited so long to strip down that he couldn't get his sweats off before the second runner came in. So there was the second man, another tiny ninth grader named Carlos Quintero or something, standing there with his thumb up his ass waiting for dopey Danny to get his sweats off over his spikes. Of course the sweats got caught on the shoes, so he had to untie his spikes, take them off, get his sweatpants off, and then put his spikes back on and tie them again. But by then, one of the laces had a knot in it, and Danny couldn't get it undone.

Fish was livid.

"Why don't you fold the fuckin' things, too?" he yelled, but no one was paying attention.

So, with one shoe on and one shoe off, Danny Boy grabbed the baton from a very patient Carlos and set off on his journey. He didn't get very far before he tripped over himself and sent the stick clattering to the track. Everybody thought this was just hilarious except for Fish who failed to see the humor in it. The whole thing was so pathetic that Fish told the anchor guy, a Haitian sophomore named Phillipe St. Jean or Jean St. Phillipe or something, not to even bother. The kid looked a little peeved that he wasn't going to run, but Coach Cahill told him that they'd stick him in another race, which seemed to pacify him some. Except for all of that, the meet was a rousing success. With one event left, the mile relay, Westfield had won a grand total of zero medals. That was when Fish decided to address the troops.

"Gentlemen, we have been here for four and a half hours," he said, his voice edging towards sarcasm. "We have wasted a beautiful afternoon and we have no medals to show for it;

that's not an easy thing to do. At this particular track meet they give away five sets of medals in every freakin' event, and we have taken zilch - zero – nada - none. I don't know if that's ever been done before, but we may be making history here – and not in a good way. There is only one event left, the mile relay, and we are going to win a medal or die trying." Fish's eyes were blazing now. "The team is Frankie, Russ, Avi, and Cam, in that order. If we medal, all is forgiven. If we don't, the whole team runs home from here. That's the deal."

Now, it was a safe bet that in the whole history of track and field other teams had gone to meets and come home empty-handed, but it certainly wasn't that common. And, while it was only about four miles back to school, some of the guys were going to have trouble making it, even if they didn't get lost on the way. It may not have even been legal to make your team run home, but Fish had that look in his eye that said, "I'm not bullshittin' here," and Pell was standing next to him with those big arms folded across his chest, so the relay decided that they'd better run fast. If they made the whole team run home, they'd never hear the end of it - so much for no pressure.

The team was in the first heat, with all of the big boys, probably because there were only eight teams entered. As the sixth seed, they drew lane two which was a break because with the staggered start they might be able to sneak up on somebody. The gun exploded and Frankie went out hard, being careful not to use up too much energy in the early rush. Coming into the second straightaway, he accelerated past a couple of teams and handed off to Russell in third place.

Now Russ, who was only a tenth grader, was jumpy to start with and Fish's threat hadn't eased his mind any. He burst out like he was shot from a cannon and was in serious trouble halfway around the track. Rigging up horribly, he was passed by four teams as he staggered home. When he handed off to Avi we were sitting in seventh, two places behind the last medal.

Unwilling to repeat Russ's mistake, Avi went out way too slowly. Running easily, he was content to hold his position until challenged. When the team behind him came up, he accelerated and when they fell back he slowed. In this manner, he ran a nice, comfortable leg that accomplished absolutely nothing. Cam got the stick still in seventh, with our medal chances fading fast.

Now Cam had all the makings of a great quarter-miler, except that he hated the race. He was six-one and 160-pounds of muscle, Jamaican, lean, and hard. He also had that long, silky stride that gobbled up ground and plenty of foot speed to go with it. The problem was that he didn't like pain, and the quarter is for masochists. He would have been perfectly happy running the one, two, and four by one, and he was fast enough to do it. But he was easily our best quarter man, and it really was his strongest event. With the coaches screaming, "One at a time," Cam set sail after the red-clad runner in sixth. Driving down the backstretch, he caught him on the second turn and then fixed his gaze on the blue-shirted Kingsbridge kid in fifth. With a twenty-meter deficit to make up and only about eighty meters left it didn't look good, but Cam didn't want to lose and he especially didn't want to run home. Hitting the afterburners, he caught the fading Royal just before the finish line and leaned across for a "close but clean" fifth.

Walking back to the bus with bronze medals dangling from their necks, Frankie turned to Cam.

"Man, I didn't think you were gonna get him."

"Shit, ah coulda run fasta if I had ta."

"You were holdin' back?"

"Jus' a lickle."

"Why?"

"'Cause ah was tinkin', if ah do more Fish gonna wan' more. Pretty soon mi runnin' di 800's, and ah won't be avin' dat. Ja-mai-can runnas ah sprintas, mon - tur-a-breds. Distance races ah fa crazee white bwoys and Af-ri-cans. Don' be tellin' Fish now, but ah got a lickle bit maw lef' en da tank."

"I won't," Frankie said, but he sure was happy to hear it.

Chapter 31

Today was Palm Sunday, which meant church and dinner at Grandma's. Fish's mother lived halfway across town in an old two-story colonial. She had been widowed for more than twenty years, Big Andy having passed away just before the first grandchild was born. Now in her early eighties and with no one left in the house to dote on, she did her best to spoil her grandkids, rationalizing, "When they go home, their parents can discipline them."

Needless to say, Fish's kids loved their grandma.

The Palm Sunday menu was an unchanging and hallowed Fischetti tradition. First came the antipasto: salami, pepperoni, prosciutto, cheese, black olives, artichoke hearts, and roasted red peppers. There were always a few loaves of crusty Italian bread, too – from D'Angelo's bakery not the supermarket. Then, after Fish had fought unsuccessfully with the kids to not get full too fast, the macaroni was served.

In keeping with custom, linguine was the pasta of choice. Drenched in the sausage and braciole-laden tomato sauce that had been simmering on the stove for hours, Parmesan cheese was grated over the top. Then, a special mixture of breadcrumbs and crushed walnuts, reserved only for Palm Sundays, was added. If this wasn't heaven, it was close enough. After the pasta, everybody took a break. The guys waddled off to the living room to watch the NBA Playoffs, and the ladies cleared the table for the next course.

Broiled chicken, with plenty of lemon and garlic was up next, and delicious as it was everybody was too stuffed to eat.

"Don't worry," grandma would say. "You can have it for tomorrow."

Then it was salad time. In keeping with the old country tradition, insalata was always served towards the end of the meal, but this dinner wasn't over yet…not by a long shot.

Apples and oranges magically appeared, soon to be joined by pecans, almonds, and roasted hazelnuts. Finally, there was a big pot of coffee, milk for the kids, and plenty of pastries and homemade Italian cheesecake. Five hours and 15,000 calories later, the Fischetti clan departed.

It had been a really nice day – good food, good company, and not a word about track. That was a good thing, too; tomorrow was Greenmont.

Chapter 32

The Greenmont meet was at home which was usually fun, but not today. That's because, first, there was actually a small crowd watching, and, second, Westfield got demolished. It was nice to think that some people had heard about the recent near victory over Brookside and were starting to take an interest, but that wasn't the truth. Usually, the only track spectators were a few parents and maybe a stray girlfriend or two. Today about 150 people were hanging around, most of them waiting for the start of the big lacrosse game against Holy Redeemer. Lacrosse always drew a good crowd; people thought it was classy and cool. And, there was no denying the macho factor; violence sells. The most violent thing at a track meet is some fat kid throwing an iron ball around. To most people, track is boring; kids run around in endless circles and nobody knows the score. Even baseball drew bigger crowds than track, and Westfield's baseball team was awful.

Anyway, the Greenmont meet was a disaster. They were probably the most talented team in the league, although they were thin in a couple of places and pretty undisciplined. They just used their superior speed to dominate the sprints, hurdles, and jumps, and didn't worry too much about anything else. It was basically a replay of the meet with Franklin North but by a bigger score. Frankie and Cam grabbed some points, and the distance team had a little success, but Green Griffin sweeps in the 100, jumps, and relays sealed the deal. The Wildcats were zero and three now and sinking fast.

Chapter 33

Both the length of Oscar's throws and the size of his waistline were increasing rapidly. Despite the best efforts of the coaches, and especially Pell who was now his nutritionist as well as landlord, the Big O continued to take his comfort in food.

Three breakfast burritos led to a package of Reese's peanut butter cups at ten o'clock. These preceded a double lunch, usually burgers and fries courtesy of the friendly neighborhood lunch ladies, followed by a pre-practice snack of Ring-Dings and a soda. If he thought no one was looking, Oscar would even try to sneak something in at practice. Pell busted him with cookie crumbs on his face and chips in his pocket one day and made him run a couple of laps, but for Oscar the punishment was just the price of doing business. Walking back to Pell's place after practice, he liked to sneak a stop at Hunan Garden to get a container of pork-fried rice. Then he would have a big dinner, and wander off later to get some ice cream, always ice cream, before going to bed. With his daily caloric intake approaching that of a small South American village, it was no wonder that Oscar was pushing three and a half bills.

But, after his epic run his personality had done a complete one-eighty. Basking in the newfound love everyone showered on him, Oscar was a changed man. Blaring hip-hop and reggaeton from his huge boom box, he now led the team in "dance warm-ups" before every practice. And, who even knew he could dance? Maybe that class he was taking was doing some good, because even the coaches had to laugh at the grinning giant with the quick feet who shimmied and shook to the pounding beat.

In Fish's words, "He looked like an epileptic bowl of Jell-o," and Oscar's signature move, "El Terremoto" (The Earthquake), was a showstopper. At the end of the last song, Oscar would go into a full-body convulsion, with everyone backing away to a safe distance. Then, he would jump as high as he could before slamming down to the ground chest first. The resulting tremor usually registered about a five on the Richter scale.

Under Pell's tutoring, his throwing was really improving, too. His shot was pretty consistent in the low forties now, and he was staying in the circle more often. Even the disc was coming along. He wasn't spinning in meets yet, preferring to punch to avoid fouls, but his nimble feet and quick arm showed promise.

It was his overeating that was the problem. In the absence of a father figure, Oscar had latched onto Pell, leaning on him for advice about pretty much everything. Pell, in turn, had confided in Fish, trying to find the secret to curb Oscar's ravenous appetite. One day, they hit upon an idea.

"I saw an ad in the *Pennysaver* today," Fish started. "It's for something called Hypnotherapy. The ad says that it can help people with all kinds of problems: smoking, overeating, all kinds of phobias. What do you think?"

"For who, Oscar?" Pell asked.

"No, for me. Who else? We got anybody else that size?"

"I don't know. It sounds dangerous - and expensive."

"Dangerous? He's dangerous now. If he fell on anyone he'd crush him. And, how much can it be? The ad says, 'Results in one session.' It's worth a shot. If we don't do something, he might explode; he's gettin' bigger by the day."

"And you think his mother's gonna go for this? There's no way she's got coverage."

"How's she gonna know? Nobody's gonna tell her."

"You want to take Oscar to a shrink, put him under a spell, and not tell his mother?"

"Not a shrink, not a spell, and somethin' like that."

"You're nuts! They'll fire you and probably me too, just for knowing you. How are you planning to pay for all this?"

"We'll talk to the guy, work something out."

"There's no way this can be legal."

"Maybe we'll bring Avi, too – cure his aversion to winning."

"Another splendid idea."

"I think so," Fish grinned. "We'll get a twofer."

Chapter 34

Since today was the last day of school before spring break, there was only a short practice to get everyone home early. Fish was on the phone with Doctor Morris Traube of the Westfield Hypnotherapy Center five minutes after the workout finished up.

"Dr. Traube? Hi, this is Angelo Fischetti; I work over at Westfield High School."

"Good afternoon. Mr…. Furschetti was it?" Doctor Traube asked.

"Yes," Fish replied, ignoring the mispronunciation. "I'm actually the track coach at Westfield."

"Oh, very good, then. How can I be of service to you?"

"Well, I'm having kind of a problem with two of my athletes. I was thinking that you might be able to help them."

"What kind of a problem are we talking about?"

"One of them has an eating disorder, and the other one is phobic."

"All right then. And, exactly what kind of eating disorder does this young man have?"

"Basically, he eats everything in sight."

Dr. Traube laughed. "I see; I guess that could be a problem. Well, hypnotherapy has proven to be very effective in modifying certain behaviors."

"That's what I've heard. So, I saw your ad and decided to give you a call."

"What's the other boy phobic about?"

"Everything"

"Everything?"

"Pretty much so. But, specifically, he's afraid to win races, even though he's better than everybody else. I'm sure it's all mixed up with his crazy family and his weird childhood, but we don't have about ten years to delve into all that."

"How much time do we have?"

"A couple of weeks."

"Oh my! Well, we'd better make an appointment then."

"I was hoping you'd say that," Fish replied.

Chapter 35

It was the first day of Spring Vacation, but there was still practice. With no meet scheduled for Easter weekend, the coaches took the opportunity to ramp up the workload even more. As soon as the final rep was done, Fish ushered

Oscar and Avi to the waiting Trackmobile and off they went to meet Dr. Traube.

They found his office pretty easily since it was right on Main Street in the middle of town and had an oversized yellow sign in front that announced, "Westfield Hypnotherapy Center."

Fish walked in first with his reluctant charges trailing. The pretty, young receptionist had them sign in and fill out some forms before telling Dr. Traube that his two o'clocks had arrived.

The good doctor, a short, chubby, rumpled-looking man with Ben Franklin glasses perched on the tip of his nose, showed them into his office.

"Make yourselves comfortable; everybody grab a chair," he said cheerfully.

Fish made the introductions.

"Dr. Traube…Oscar Amaya and Avi Glick."

"Pleased to meet you boys," the doctor replied. "Your coach has told me some nice things about you."

The meeting lasted half-an-hour and went halfway well.

Astonishingly, Oscar seemed almost too accepting to most of Dr. Traube's suggestions. Agreeable by nature, the big boy must have known deep down that his eating was way out of control and that he had to change. Despite his six-four frame, he was far too heavy, and his childhood nickname of "Gordito" had long since lost its charm.

Avi, though, was another story completely. Since he was afraid of virtually everything, it was no shock that doctors were high on his list. And, like Oscar, he was eighteen years old and didn't need parental consent to get treatment. Not surprisingly, convincing him to go hadn't been easy, as Fish had found out when he'd cornered him in the reference section of the school library one rainy Tuesday afternoon.

"C'mon Avi, what have you got to lose?" Fish asked after outlining his plan.

"Everything," Avi muttered. "I don't want to go; I hate doctors."

"He's not even a real medical doctor; he's a hypnotherapist."

"A hippo what?"

"Not hippo - hypno. He's a hypnotherapist, like a hypnotist. He can take away your fears and anxieties."

"How?"

"By getting you to relax. He'll put your mind at ease so doubts won't creep in when you're running – or taking a test."

"I don't think so. It sounds weird."

"Oscar's going to go, too."

"Why? What's he afraid of?"

"Nothing, but you've probably noticed that he has a bit of a weight problem. Dr. Traube's going to help him with that."

"How?"

"By getting him to realize that he doesn't need to eat all the time."

"I don't know," Avi said again.

Fish rubbed his chin slowly, considering his next move.

"Listen, you read science fiction don't you?"

"Yeah."

"You ever read Robert Heinlein?"

"Yeah, all the time."

"You know the story 'Elsewhen'?"

"No"

"I'll give it to you, then. It's about these people who control their destinies through their minds – through hypnosis."
"Yeah?"
"Yeah. And, their destinies are really their deepest desires."
"Cool. I'll do it."
"Do what? See the doctor?"
"No! Read 'Elsewhere.'"
"'Elsewhen,'" Fish corrected. "How 'bout the doctor?"
"I want to read the story first."
"Fair enough," Fish sighed.

And so, eventually, Avi read the story and halfheartedly agreed to see the doctor.

As Dr. Traube later revealed, Oscar was a prime hypnotherapy candidate because on some level he really did want to change. Once he was fully relaxed, it was a fairly simple matter for him to envision a new Oscar…"Oscar Suave"… a young man capable of winning track meets, dance contests, and the hearts of pretty senoritas everywhere. In his deep subconscious, Oscar was already rejecting Big Macs, fries, and Pepsis. Instead, he was enjoying fresh salads, crisp apples, and sparkling water. When he left the office, both he and Dr. Traube were smiling broadly.

"Oscar should do well with this program," Dr. Traube confided to Fish. "He's tired of being 'Fatso;' he's ready to be somebody else."

Avi…well… not so much. Truth be told, he wasn't ready or willing to be anyone else – even though that was bound to be an improvement.

Abraham Lincoln once said, "Most people are just about as happy as they make up their minds to be," and that pretty much described Avi, as long as you substituted the word "unhappy" for "happy." Despite reading the story Fish had recommended and showing up for the first hypnotherapy appointment, Avi wasn't buying in. He couldn't relax, wouldn't talk about his problems, and wasn't capable of visualizing any kind of success. When Dr. Traube asked him to imagine himself winning a big race and standing proudly on the victory stand with a gold medal around his neck, all Avi could do was laugh derisively and mumble, "Yeah, right."

They left the office around three in the afternoon, one boy smiling, one boy frowning, and one coach looking rather perplexed.

Chapter 36

Even though it was the day before Easter, there was still a ten o'clock practice. And when some of the guys started grumbling about it, Fish was quick to nip the insurrection in the bud.

"What are you guys bellyachin' about?" he asked. "Didn't I give you off yesterday?"

"Yeah, but it was Good Friday," McDermott complained. "And I'm a good Catholic boy."

"You're not a good anything," Fish shot back. "And Good Friday's a day of sacrifice, a time to fast and repent. What'd you do? I'll bet you didn't even go to church. Did you pray the rosary? I'd hate to think you wasted the whole day."

McDermott just looked puzzled.

"It's Passover, too," Avi interrupted. "We should get time off for that. You're being anti…anti…"

"Semitic?" Jacobson offered.

"Yeah, anti-Semitic," Avi finished. "I'm telling my rabbi."

"Tell your rabbi; tell your mother and your father, too. You can put it in the freakin' *Jewish Press* for all I care." Fish was rolling now. "Besides, isn't Passover eight days long?"

"Yeah"

"And this is a middle day, right?"

"Uh huh; I think so."

"So what's the big deal? When did you suddenly get so religious?"

It was funny how guys who broke The Ten Commandments all year long suddenly got devout when they thought it might get them out of practice.

"An' 'ow 'bout da Rastas?" Cam tried. "We gotta pray an' ra-pent, too."

"What are you smokin'?" Fish politely inquired. "Oh wait, you're a Rasta so I guess I know the answer to that. But, aren't you actually a Protestant? Your mother runs that prayer group over at the Church of God on Preston Street, doesn't she?"

Cam grinned; he knew when he was busted.

"So, if you guys would kindly get back to work," Fish suggested, "maybe we can all go home and actually celebrate the holidays."

After practice, Fish had a laundry list of things to do: hit King Kullen to buy groceries for his mother, fix the leaky faucet in the downstairs bathroom, pick up the Easter dessert for tomorrow, and do some track entries on the computer. All he wanted to do, though, was go home and take a nap.

He got the food first and dropped it off. Then he went home to grab a quick bite. No one was around, so he made himself a turkey, lettuce, and tomato sandwich, grabbed the newspaper, propped his feet up on the coffee table, and leaned back on the couch.

Two hours later, when the crew returned from shopping, the faucet was still dripping, dessert was nowhere to be found, and the computer was asleep. So was Fish, snoring peacefully with the sandwich and the paper resting comfortably on his lap.

Chapter 37

On Easter Sunday, after the Fischettis got back from church, it was time for the annual Easter Egg Hunt. "The Hunt" had started years ago, when the kids were little, as a pleasant springtime frolic. By now it had morphed into a more violent version of Wrestlemania.

On the night before Easter, Fish and his wife would hide exactly fifty-two plastic eggs around the house. There were always fifty-two because Fish was into symbolism, one egg for each week of the year, and also because that's how many eggs they had. They filled the eggs with money. Most of them had small change inside – nickels and dimes, a quarter, maybe a half-dollar. Then there were the big cash eggs, some with a dollar, a few with five, two with ten, and one with twenty. On Easter morning, Fish would blow his old, silver-plated whistle and the kids would tear through the house in a cash-mad frenzy. If it wasn't exactly the true Easter spirit, at least it was good old-fashioned fun and everybody looked forward to it. You would think that AJ, being the oldest and strongest, would grab the most eggs, but that wasn't always the case. Maria always made a detailed study of her parents' egg-hiding history and pored over her charts during Holy Week. She would even find some eggs that her parents had forgotten. And Matty, because of his slight build, found the odd eggs, the ones hidden in shoes, on chair seats, and under tables. When the dust had settled, everyone except Fish was about twenty bucks richer.

Another family custom was to barbecue on Easter – no matter the weather. Most of the time this wasn't a problem, but today it was. Because Easter is a moveable feast, it can fall anywhere from the end of March to late April. Although this year's holiday was pretty late, the weather obviously hadn't gotten the memo. The temperature had dropped sharply throughout the day, and the leaden sky promised snow.

Around four-thirty Fish fired up the old Webber and grabbed the two-inch-thick filet mignons his wife had bought at Pat the Butcher's. A thin sheet of slush covered the ground, and flakes were falling fast, but tradition is tradition.

"You can't barbecue outside; the steaks will get wet," his wife warned. "I'll do them in here."

"Nah, don't worry. The fire'll be hot, and I'll put the grill in the garage."

"You'll suffocate in there. I can do them under the broiler just as well."

"It'll be okay; I'll leave the door open. Plus, it wouldn't be the same. We do 'em outside every year."

"You know," she said, "you don't always have to do things the same way."

"Yeah, I do."

"Why?"

"Because it's tradition. It's like eating turkey and cranberry sauce on Thanksgiving and having the seven fishes on

Christmas Eve. You want to change those things, too? You don't mess with tradition."

"What do you think would happen if you changed?"

"I don't know, and I'm not gonna find out."

"You're just afraid of change."

"No, I'm not."

"Yes, you are. Name one thing that you've changed recently."

Fish thought for about ten seconds until his eyes lit up.

"My underwear," he grinned, "just this morning."

Chapter 38

The freak spring snow had melted as quickly as it had come, which was a good thing since today called for a home meet against the neighboring Taneoke Braves. The team swept the last of the slush off the track and set up the hurdles. Then they went into the gym to stay warm, stretch, and wait for their opponents.

The Braves were a middle-of-the-road team like most of the league. They weren't exactly pushovers, but they lacked any real talent or depth. Once upon a time the "Border War" between Taneoke and Westfield had meant something, but that was back in the day. Now it was just another track meet.

"We're oh and three," Fish announced before the meet, which wasn't exactly breaking news, "and, that's not very good. And, Taneoke is one and two, so they're thinkin' the same way we are – that this is a chance to pick up a win. I know on their bus, right now, their coach is saying the same things I am. It's just going to be a question of who wants it more. They've got some good guys, but so do we. They have a couple of sprinters and jumpers, but not too much in the distances and weights, so it should be close." Fish finished by leading the, "One-Two-Three, Westfield," cheer, and screaming, "Let's get out there and show 'em what we got."

So Westfield did, but it wasn't much. Taneoke dominated the sprints, despite Cam's best efforts, and even Frankie's firsts in both hurdles couldn't stem the tide. Their mediocre distance runners beat Simmons and McDermott, and Avi, who'd been totally dazed and confused since last week's encounter with Dr. Traube, had a truly dreadful day. He finished dead last in the mile and then dropped out of the deuce, even though he was leading by plenty with only two laps to go.

Fish just looked at him kinda bewildered before asking quite seriously, "Avi, are you on drugs?"

Avi didn't even answer, which Fish may have taken as a "yes." He simply wandered away while Fish sadly shook his head.

"Don't worry about the relay," Fish yelled after him. "Why don't you just go over by the tree and rest for awhile?"

The jumpers got waxed pretty badly too, with only Howley providing anything good. The one true highlight of the meet came in the weights where Oscar had his best day yet. Smiling from ear to ear, he won the shot with a 45'1" PR and then took second in the disc with another best, this time at 123' even. When Fish congratulated him, he proudly announced that it was all due to his new diet; he had already lost five pounds and was proud of it. When he lifted his shirt to prove it, Fish mumbled something about a deck chair and the *Titanic* that nobody understood. The ridiculous sight of Oscar's jelly-belly flopping around was the only good laugh of the day.

Chapter 39

"We need a jumper – bad; I'm serious. There's got to be one kid in this whole goddamned school that can actually jump," Fish complained to his assistants after practice the next day. But nobody had an answer.

"Josh, what's the problem with these guys?" Fish asked. "They're killin' us every meet."

"The fact is they're not very good," Coach Olson replied. "They know what to do; that's not the issue. They've just got no pop, no ups. You remember that movie with Woody Harrelson and Wesley Snipes, *White Men Can't Jump*? That's us."

"But we're not even that white," Fish countered. "How about Jamal Reed, he looks like a high jumper?"

"Looks can be deceiving; he's too stiff – can't bend."

"And Gideon Barber?"

"He should take up the trumpet," Olson continued. "Too erratic – he needs a GPS to find his takeoff spot. Sometimes he's a foot away and sometimes he's five feet out. Did you know he missed the whole pit the other day… and that's a big pit?"

"He get hurt?"

"Nah, he landed on his head, didn't feel a thing. How about your guys? You've got the long and triplers; anything there?"

"Not much – too small, too slow, and too stupid. I'm the only one who knows what to do, and I can't jump anymore. This is gonna sound crazy, but if we had one good jumper we could make a little noise at the League Meet."

"That IS crazy," Olson protested.

"No, really. Look, the Leagues are scored differently than the duals, right?"

"Yeah, so?"

"In the dual meets you have to cover all the events, but in the Leagues all you need are a few good guys. The scoring is ten-eight-six-four-two-one. If you take enough big points, you can win."

"Uh…hel-lo!" Pell cut in. "We're oh and four, and we just got our asses kicked by Taneoke, who got their asses kicked by Greenmont, who got their asses kicked by Kingsbridge. That's a lot of ass kickin' and we're not doin' any of it."

"Listen, we've got Cam in the two and the four, and Frankie in both hurdles, that's four good events," Fish replied.

"Out of seventeen," Pell added. "That makes thirteen bad ones."

"Then, we've got Howley and Jakes in the vault; they'll score some."

"Yeah, and…."

"And Oscar is starting to come on in both throws; he could do something, too."

"So?"

"And, the relay; we can score in the four by four."

"You're dreaming," Pell scoffed. "It's a seven-team meet, right?"

"Yeah."

"We'll be lucky to get fourth."

"Pell's right," Cahill agreed. "Kingsbridge, Greenmont, North Franklin, and Taneoke - in that order. We're maybe fifth– at best."

"We just need one jumper," Fish persisted.

"Yeah - Carl Lewis. And, another sprinter, another weight man, and, oh yeah, a distance guy who doesn't quit in the middle of every fuckin' race," Pell suggested.

"Yeah, those things, too," Fish conceded.

Chapter 40

Avi was even more nervous than usual today. He had three tests: math, which he sort of liked but wasn't very good at; history, which he didn't like and was pretty bad at; and Spanish, which he hated and was horrible at. Everything in his life was royally screwed up. He was doing terribly in school, his running had reached a new low, and when he had tried to talk to the cute sophomore girl who was his locker neighbor, his stuttering had taken over and he could only stammer, "Hhhhhiiiii," like a crazed Samurai, before she fled in terror. He couldn't talk to his parents who were busy working and doting on his successful siblings, and he couldn't talk to his siblings who were busy being successful and doted upon.

Math was first period and the test wasn't hard, but Avi's nerves kicked in and he couldn't remember anything he had studied. Formulas, functions, and rules got all mixed-up, and he knew he hadn't done well at all.

"Maybe a sixty, if I'm lucky," he thought.

He could hear his father moaning already, "Avi, I'm an accountant, how can you be so bad in math?"

"Leave him alone Marvin," his mother would answer. "Have a little more pot roast, Avi. Then maybe you'll take a nice nap."

But the answer wasn't in pot roast or in napping. History was period seven, and even though he'd looked over his notes at lunch he couldn't keep the names and dates straight. The Articles of Confederation, Constitution, Declaration and Bill of Rights all merged into one huge, confounding document. Did anyone actually care about the third amendment? And what about Marbury versus Madison? Did anyone even know who they were? He sure as hell didn't. By the time ninth period Spanish rolled around, Avi was "muy loco." He couldn't face the irregular verbs and subordinate clauses that lay in wait, so he fell back on his usual strategy – he went to the nurse.

Westfield's nurse, Liz Loughlin, was nearing retirement and decidedly old school, but she still liked kids.

"Avi, this is the third time you've been here this week," she stated. "What's the problem now?"

"I don't know; my head hurts."

"Your head?"

"And my stomach."

"Anything else?"

"Maybe my throat?"

"Maybe?"

"Yeah, my throat, too."

"Did you have any tests today?"

"Two."

"Do you have one this period?"

"I dunno; maybe."

"That means you do. You know that these symptoms of yours are all psychosomatic, right?"

"What's that mean? I'm a psycho?"

"No, it means that your illnesses aren't real; they're all in your head."

"I told you, that's what hurts."

Nurse Loughlin laughed.

"That's because you're nervous or upset about something. There's nothing wrong with your head or your stomach or anything else. You just need to talk to somebody and find out what's really bothering you. Then you'll feel better. Lie down on that cot over there and rest for a while. I'll let your teacher know that you're here."

As he moved towards the cot, Avi slid his hand into his back pocket. Dr. Traube's card was still there.

Chapter 41

Practice was actually fun today…finally. The coaches had been promising a break for a long time, but somehow they never got around to it. Anyway, with another invite on tap for tomorrow, today was as good a day as any.

Fish put everybody out on the football field and divided the group into two teams: the Greens and the Golds. The sprinters and hurdlers were Greens, and the distance runners and jumpers were Golds. The weight guys were split evenly between the two squads because they couldn't run much, and the sides had to be fair. Then Fish pulled a brand new soccer ball from his bottomless track bag and marched to the fifty-yard line. The soccer goals and nets were still up, and the lines on the field were somewhat visible, so with the coaches serving as officials the first Green and Gold World Cup kicked off. Since the stakes were pretty high, the losers had to buy lunch for the winners at tomorrow's meet, the guys were playing for keeps.

As the Green captain, Frankie decided to go for broke. The Greens had a big advantage in speed, so they attacked from the opening whistle. Cam, who had played plenty of soccer back in Jamaica, was their unquestioned star. Besides having blazing speed, he could actually dribble and pass, skills that none of his teammates possessed. But after about ten minutes and several fruitless scoring chances, fatigue took hold and the superior stamina of the distance guys kicked in. They came in waves, led by Andy Simmons a half-miler who had played two years of JV soccer. Frankie had put Oscar in goal, thinking that his sheer bulk would reduce the shooting area for their opponents, but the big boy, who had grown up watching and playing futbol with his uncles and cousins, had no desire to stay put. He rampaged around the backline, directing his teammates, shouting encouragement, and making a series of dazzling saves. On one corner kick, he barreled out of the goal, knocked down friend and foe alike, and punched the ball clear over the sideline. After thirty minutes of non-stop action, and with the game still scoreless, Fish decided it was halftime and we everyone collapsed on the ground.

"A'right, mon, enuf a dis fool-ish-ness," Cam complained. "Gimme di damn ball and wheel win di game; ah don' wanna be buyin' dem bwoyz lunch tomarra."

"We'd like to," Frankie said, "but you may have noticed that we seem to be having a little trouble getting it out of our own end."

"Jus av da beeg boy punta down. Oscah kin keeck id da 'hole way."

"O-man, can you do that?" Frankie asked.

"Sure, I think so. We're gonna have the wind this half, too."

So that was the strategy for the second half – "Boot and Scoot," and it nearly paid off. With about a minute left and the game still "nil - nil," Oscar bashed one nearly the length of the field to Cam, who was flying down the right wing. He faked a helpless high jumper out of his shoes and stormed to the goal on a forty-five degree angle. When he was about fifteen yards away, the defense closed down, and he let loose a right-footed rocket. The goalie, a tall, skinny discus thrower named Kravitz, had no chance, but he got lucky. The ball cracked off the crossbar like a rifle shot and rebounded nearly to midfield where the Golds began their counterattack. When a long shot bounced off the Green defense for a corner kick, Fish announced, "Ten seconds left – last play of the game."

Simmons took the left side corner and lofted a high floater that seemed to hover forever in front of the Green goal. Oscar charged out hard, but the ball eluded his straining fingertips and drifted across the goalmouth where it caromed perfectly off the forehead of one unknowing and oblivious Avi Glick and into the far corner of the goal. Avi, who had been quietly uninvolved for the entire sixty minutes, had no clue as to what had just happened but everyone else did. As he stood there ruefully rubbing his head, his jubilant teammates hoisted him onto their shoulders and carried him off the field.

As they headed towards the locker room, they were chanting loudly, "FREE LUNCH! FREE LUNCH! FREE LUNCH!"

Chapter 42

The mood on the bus was decidedly upbeat on Saturday. Everyone was present and accounted for by eight-thirty sharp, and instead of the usual bunch of sullen grumps, the bus was filled with chattering teenagers still buzzing about Avi's improbable goal. Oscar had dubbed it, "The Head of God," in tribute to Maradona's miraculous World Cup score, and Avi was actually smiling for a change, although he kept apologizing that he didn't score on purpose.

The bus was headed to Spruce Valley for a middle-sized invitational that drew about twenty-five schools. With a spanking new track and a renewed interest in the sport, Spruce Valley was starting to make its mark in Track and Field. Although their team wasn't fully up to speed yet, their meet was and from an athlete's point of view all good invitationals had a few things in common.

First, they should have a nice level of competition – not too much and not too little. If the competition is too fierce, like at Penn Relays or someplace, it's no fun. You're beaten before you start because there's no hope of winning anything.

But if the competition is too weak, victory is meaningless because you didn't beat anybody good. Like in that story "The Three Bears," the competition at Spruce Valley was "just right."

Second, good Saturday meets should be coed. Some crusty, old dinosaurs like Fish don't like boy-girl meets because they take all day. And, that part is true. There are always about six heats of the Girls 4 X 800 relay that take up more than an hour and give everybody a chance to grab a bite to eat, but it's still nice to have the ladies around. They make the time go faster, and with so many schools there you can always scope out the hotties and get some numbers. Cam was the unquestioned master of this with his short dreads, cool shades, and silver tongue. He considered anything less than five new names and digits at a meet a total failure. Then, he would spend the whole bus ride home calling or texting all his newbies, just to let them know he was "tinkin' 'bout dem."

In fact, Oscar was becoming quite the lady's man, too. He could "shake, shake, shake" all day, and with his massive radio blasting all the little girls would gyrate around him like he was a giant Maypole. Then Rodney Hawthorne, another fat-boy shot putter would yell, "THERE'S AN EARTHQUAKE A COMIN'," and Oscar, to great acclaim, would perform "El Terremoto." It was a guaranteed crowd pleaser. When Fish told him one time that a Maypole was really an ancient fertility symbol of a giant penis, Big O just smiled slyly and nodded his head.

The last thing a good Saturday meet needs is "logistics." That means that the host school shouldn't be too far away, and it should have a fast track, good food, and plenty of port-a-potties. This last point is vastly underrated because high school tracks are always way out in a godforsaken field somewhere far from any buildings. Before meets started renting portable toilets, athletes had to run about half a mile to go to the bathroom and then another half-mile back. That took too long and it was tiring, especially if nature called just before your event. Some guys used to try and hide behind trees to pee, but too many of them got caught and got in trouble. Port-a-potties all have dopey names like "Call A Head" and "Johnny On The Spot," but at least they put them right near the track now. And, another plus is that girls rarely use them because they're pretty gross, so there are rarely any lines. The potties are quite vile, but who cares – no one's going to eat a sandwich in there. Although, Oscar may have done that a few times before his recent conversion. Anyway, Spruce Valley had all of the important amenities so it was a very popular meet.

Oh yeah, the team did a little better, too. Frankie won the intermediates, running a PR fifty-eight three, and Cam took enough time out from his pursuit of females to win the quarter in a tick over fifty. The O man continued his meteoric rise, medaling in the shot and disc and then proudly pinning both medals onto his uniform top for the rest of the meet and the bus ride home. Pell told him that he looked like one of those Mexican generals from the *Zorro* movies, but Oscar didn't bat an eye. And even Avi, buoyed by his recent soccer success, got into the act by snagging the last medal in the two-mile. Although he probably should have done better, as Fish astutely pointed out, "At least he didn't stop running this time."

Chapter 43

Another Monday - another meet – another defeat. It sounded like one of those stupid Japanese haikus they teach in junior English and it was getting old fast.

Today it was Kingsbridge, the perennial league power, at their place. The WASPiest school in the league, the Royals (Hear! Hear!) prided themselves on tradition and on doing things "The Kingsbridge Way," which basically meant buying success, no matter what the cost. Located in an affluent suburb that was way leafier than Westfield, their student body exited million dollar homes clad in Abercrombie and J.Crew and drove to school in shiny new Lexuses and Audis. At Westfield, the kids lived in rented apartments, wore bargain store jeans and t-shirts, and either walked to school or rode the bus.

Their facilities were top notch too, with brand new lights surrounding the football field and recently refurbished bleachers ringing the royal blue, polyurethane Tartan track. Their coaches were the best that money could buy, with their soccer coach having been imported from England, their swimming coach from Australia, and their track coach from Eastern Europe. And, Head Track Coach Pavel Hirtek had the foresight to bring a few choice athletes with him, namely the Danicic twins, Josef and Tomas, who spelled double trouble in Serbo-Croatian or any other language you could think of. Jo-Dan was an excellent sprinter-hurdler who could run anything up to the 400, and To-Dan was a terrific jumper who was equally adept in the high, long, and triple. Together, they were fully capable of scoring sixty points in any given meet. That was enough to worry about, but Kingsbridge had more - much more. Liam Healy, a foreign-exchange student from Ireland who had mysteriously decided to stay at Kingsbridge for his senior year, led their distance team. Coincidentally, he also happened to be the reigning Irish Junior Cross Country Champion. And, they had a big-time thrower in Ryan Corneau, their three-hundred-pound All County defensive tackle, who had developed into a fifty-foot shot putter. They were going to be a handful for sure.

And aside from all that, they hated Westfield and Westfield hated them right back. The nastiness had started a long time ago when Westfield had the nerve to actually beat Kingsbridge in some football game, breaking their winning streak of about a million in a row. Kingsbridge claimed that the refs had cost them the game, but that was just sour grapes. They couldn't accept the fact that they simply got beat, and that it was Westfield that had done the beating. They truly believed that winning was their birthright. Kingsbridge kids were born rich, raised rich, got rich, and died rich. They went to the finest schools, had tutors and personal trainers, and eventually moved on to jobs on Wall Street or with Fortune 500 companies to make millions of dollars in bonuses and stock options. Then they were free to marry other perfect people and start the whole deranged cycle all over again. That's how it had been for generations, and the Kingsbridge crew wanted it to stay exactly that way. Nobody else did, though, so it wasn't just Westfield – everybody despised them.

Therefore, it shouldn't have been a total shock when a neatly-lettered white banner with blue printing greeted the bus upon its arrival at the baronial high school gates.

"Kingsbridge Royals Dump Westfield Trash!" it proclaimed.

Everybody went crazy. Some of the guys, led by the vaulters, wanted to rip the banner down, and Fish probably would have let them, except it was hung about twenty feet high between a tree and a light pole and would have required some serious climbing to get to. Fish said to use it as motivation and pointedly reminded everyone that Westfield hadn't won on Kingsbridge's track in ten years.

"Once they lower the drawbridge so we can cross the fuckin' moat," he began, "this might be a good time to start showin' 'em something."

He was using his medium-level sarcasm that managed to get everyone's attention and still piss them off at the same time.

One of the freshmen, Brandon somebody, timidly raised his little hand.

"Why don't we ever win here?" he asked.

"Good question, Brandon," Fish replied. "Would anyone like to answer him?"

"Because they're really good?" Simmons offered.

"They don't like to be losin' to us?" Greenie chimed in.

"Everybody here's rich and we're poor?" Avi tried.

Fish's face got a little redder with each response.

"You're all right," he snapped. "They are good, they don't like losing, and they're rich as hell, but that's not why they beat us. They beat us because they know they can. And, worse than that, we know they can. We have good athletes and we can beat them, the same as we can beat any other team – but we don't think we can."

Since his team hadn't beaten anybody yet, no one was sure if Fish really believed what he was saying. But some of the guys were nodding in agreement and others were staring straight ahead, steely-jawed and resolute. Maybe the banner or Fish or something was getting to them. Maybe

Westfield could beat this powerhouse of a team that was so much better than them on paper.

And, then it became clear where Fish was going with all this. It wasn't really about this meet, or any track meet for that matter. It was all about confidence – something was in painfully short supply at Westfield. It was about believing in yourself and not worrying about the consequences. It was about going for it without fearing failure. It was about laying it all on the line for your teammates and having them do the same for you.

So, the Wildcats charged onto Kingsbridge's beautiful blue and white million-dollar track, on a picture-perfect spring afternoon, brimming with hope and bursting with energy, and proceeded to get their asses royally kicked – or at least kicked by the Royals.

The inventory of errors was impressive, starting with Frankie's tripping over the last hurdle in the intermediates and including Greenie's wandering out of his lane once again. Cam's false start in the quarter, and a dropped baton in the sprint relay added to the fiasco. Only Oscar with two strong seconds and Avi with a pair of thirds had any success.

Maybe that banner was right. The Danicic brothers won their usual six events, the meet ended with Kingsbridge laughing and joking, and the final score was a whole lot to very little. Fish didn't say much on the bus ride home; he just slumped down in his seat and whispered with Cahill, but he was definitely planning something – he had to be.

Chapter 44

There was no practice today, which happened about as often as the Mets won the World Series. Was Fish sick? He never missed a day. Was he dead? He was in school, teaching as usual. No, he wasn't sick and he wasn't dead; there was just no practice. Half the team didn't believe it and showed up after school anyway, suspecting a trick so that Fish could make them run penalty miles tomorrow. But all they found was a hand-written note taped to the locker room window that read:

"No Practice Today! Be On Time Tomorrow!"

The two exclamation points made the note seem pretty ominous, but eventually everyone got the message and took off. Some of the guys headed off to see their girlfriends, some to hang out, and some to get a head start on their homework for a change. Frankie just went home and took a nap; he didn't know what else to do.

Chapter 45

Unbeknownst to all, Avi had visited Dr. Traube twice since his last test meltdown. He had actually run a little better lately, but that was chalked up to the Law of Averages and maybe some residual effects from his soccer goal. The truth was that he had gotten so disgusted with himself that he was ready to try almost anything. So, he surrendered himself at least a little to Dr. Traube's suggestions and tried to envision himself doing well.

At first, it didn't work at all. The whole concept of success was so foreign to Avi that he couldn't even imagine it. But after a while the doctor got him to the point where he could relax a bit and picture himself running free and easy, with no negative thoughts floating around in his head. If he couldn't envision winning yet, at least he could imagine not losing.

Because distance runners have so much time to think, both in training and racing, they suffer more crises in confidence than other track athletes. In most events there is no thinking at all. Sprinters go "balls to the wall," with no strategy whatsoever, and the same is true in the field events where the actual action lasts only a few seconds. Even in the hurdles there isn't much thinking. In the intermediates there is a general plan for each race, and that plan can be adjusted, but there's no time for deep thought. In the highs, there's no thought at all; it's just muscle memory - one–two–three–dive, and repeat it ten times. Distance runners are a different breed. They're the philosophers of the track world and Avi was their Kafka. Given to dark thought and serious reflection, they have the highest grades (except for Avi), the ugliest girlfriends, and even the best of them require about four and a half minutes to run the mile and almost ten minutes to finish the deuce. It's no wonder that they're all basket cases.

In fact, Dr. Traube had put Avi into a kind of trance to get him to see his potential. He had given him a "trigger word" that he could repeat to himself to activate the positive imagery, and he had also provided a "wake-up mechanism" to snap Avi out of his reverie. Although no one knew it at the time, it was really "Hypno Avi" who had run better in the last two meets.

Chapter 46

At about one-thirty in the afternoon the English Office phone rang; Fish's wife was on the other end.

"Listen," she said, "You better go down to Matty's school again; there's some kind of problem."

"What kind of problem? And, why can't you go?" Fish wasn't big on problems, especially in the middle of a school day.

"I can't get out of school now; you know that. You can be there in ten minutes."

"I have a class comin' up. What happened?"

"It's that stupid slingshot, again. I thought you said he couldn't take it to school."

"I did."

"Well, it didn't work. According to Ms. Hazelton, the principal, he's been shooting at girls in the playground."

"Shooting at girls? Why?"

"Because he's eleven years old? Because there aren't any squirrels or birds around? I don't know. I just know that this is the third time he's gotten in trouble with that thing, and it's going in the garbage."

"Where's he shooting them?"

"I just told you - in the schoolyard."

"No, the girls…in what body part?"

"Who knows? And why does it matter? He's not even supposed to have it."

"I'll take care of it. I'm leaving right now."

Westfield Middle School was only a mile down the road, and Fish got there in a hurry. Because he had to teach in half an hour, he'd have to wrap this up quickly, but since Matty was now a three-time loser under the school's newly adopted

Code of Conduct, it might not be that simple. When Fish walked into the main office it was like the clock had been turned back forty years and he was the one in trouble again.

From behind her formidable desk, Mrs. Byrd, the principal's ancient secretary who'd been there since Fish was a kid, glowered.

"Take a seat, Mr. Fischetti," she ordered. "Ms. Hazelton will be right with you."

Fish plopped himself into one of the three straight-backed office chairs that were lined up with their backs to the hall windows. He didn't know too much about Ms. Hazelton and the little he did know he didn't like. For one thing, she was way too young to be the principal of anything – and far too pretty. Middle school principals should all look like Mrs. Byrd with her blue hair pulled up in a bun and her mouth twisted all around like she'd been sucking lemons.

Kim Hazelton materialized as if by magic.

"Hello, Mr. Fischetti. Thank you for taking time from your busy day," she began.

She was dressed in that scoop-necked top/business jacket and short skirt style that shouted, "I'm extremely professional, but I'm also hot as hell."

Fish didn't like it and he couldn't figure it out either. If she was a principal, why didn't she look like one? There was no ring on her left hand, either, which was a little surprising since she had to be in her thirties and she was very good-looking. She motioned for Fish to have a seat in the inner office and closed the door.

"I just want you to know, Mr. Fischetti, that everyone here at Westfield Middle absolutely adores Matty; he's a wonderful child," she started. "But he does seem to be having some difficulty with behavioral issues, particularly regarding his classmates."

"Cut the crap and say what you mean, buttercup," Fish thought to himself. Matty didn't have any behavioral issues; he just liked to shoot his slingshot.

"Have you noticed any aggressive behavior at home," she asked, "perhaps regarding his siblings?"

"Do you mean does he shoot his slingshot at them?" Fish shot back.

"No, not exactly," she replied evenly. "Does he act out or fight with them? Does he exhibit any overt hostility or agitation?"

"No, not that I can see," Fish said. "I mean, he fights with them about as much as any normal kid – maybe a little less because he's so damn quiet."

"Is he prone to mood swings? Any uncharacteristic outbursts?"

"No, never. He only has one mood – placid. He's about the most even-tempered kid you can imagine."

Fish glanced at his watch. Time was wasting and he had to get back for class. Geez, he was beginning to hate her.

"Well, because this is the third incident that we have had, I'm going to have to recommend that Matty sees the school psychologist."

Fish hit the ceiling.

"You're going to recommend what?"

"I'm going to recommend that he sees the school psychologist, Dr. Melissa Robertson. She's a lovely woman and an excellent clinician with many years of experience in dealing with these very types of situations. I'm sure that after a few sessions she will be able to determine the underlying causes of Matty's behavior. Then we can all meet to design and implement a comprehensive plan to remediate the problem."

"Whoa! Slow down sister. You want to send a normal eleven-year-old boy, who does very well in school I might add, to your house shrink because of a couple of playground incidents?"

"Three incidents to be exact, all involving a dangerous weapon. And, I must take exception to your tone. I just think it's prudent that we take these steps now so that in the future...."

Fish cut her off at the knees.

"I just think it would be prudent if you got your head out of your ass and smelled the fuckin' coffee."

That rather amusing construction actually made a little bit of sense.

"Leave the kid alone; he's a normal little boy," Fish argued. "I'll take away his slingshot; promise. That's it! Period! End of report!"

And with that, Fish spun out of his chair, stormed out of the office, and slammed the door behind him.

When he got back to the high school, three minutes before his next class, he called his wife.

"How did it go?" she asked.

"Oh, swimmingly," he replied. "I'll tell you all about it at dinner."

Chapter 47

It didn't take long for the shit to hit the fan. As soon as Fish went to sign in at seven-thirty the next morning, he noticed the principal's secretary, Arlene Stoffel, giving him what was known at Westfield as "The Fish Eye." This wasn't the regular, old, suspicious-looking "fish eye" that anyone could get. This was the one reserved for Fish himself when he had gone off the deep end once too often.

"Aw right, Arlene; I know that look," Fish grumbled.

"You should," she remarked. "It's named after you."

"Just give it to me straight. How pissed is the old man?"

"On a scale of one to ten?"

"Yeah"

"Nine and a half"

"Nine? I didn't do anything."

"And a half, and that's not what I heard."

Just then the principal's door opened and a tall, distinguished-looking, gray-haired man peered out.

"Mr. Fischetti, a moment of your precious time perhaps?"

Bernie Kroll had been in the Westfield schools for close to fifty years, first as a teacher and then as an administrator. In fact, he'd been principal of the high school for more than twenty of them. He'd been around longer than Fish, longer than anyone.

"Good luck," Arlene whispered as Fish entered the inner sanctum.

"What's up, Bernie?" Fish played dumb. "Good-looking day, huh?"

"Not for you," Bernie said, getting right down to business. "I got a call from Kim Hazleton yesterday."

"And how is the lovely Ms. Hazleton?" Fish asked innocently.

"Pissed off, that's how she is."

"I can explain that."

"You'd better. She said you cursed her out and threatened her. Those are very serious allegations."

"I didn't do that. Definitely not. I never threatened her; I wouldn't do that."

"So you did curse her out then?"

"No… not exactly. I may have used some…uh… flowery language when I was talking to her, but I didn't curse her out."

"You can't keep doing this stuff, Fish. She's a principal; you can't talk to her like that. It's disrespectful. And, it's not like this is the first time either." Kroll's tone had softened, but only a little.

"I didn't mean to, Bernie, but she pissed me off."

"Everybody does, that's why you're always in hot water."

"Not like her. She can't even speak English. Everything she says is couched in some kind of administrative jargon. And now she wants to send my son to the school shrink."

"Matty?"

"Yeah"

"Why?"

"Because he was shooting his slingshot at recess or something and the girls got scared."

"Did he hit any of them?"

"Nah, I don't think so."

"Then what's the big deal?'

"I dunno. I think it's the third time it's happened."

"Oh"

"Listen, he's a good kid. He's so quiet I don't know what the hell he's thinkin' half the time, but there's not a mean bone in his body. He wouldn't hurt a fly."

"Well, you know what you have to do to make this go away, right?"

"Apologize?"

"Yeah."

"Not happenin'; she was way out of line. My kid's not crazy."

"You were way out of line, too, and she outranks you."

"So? What happens if we don't kiss and make-up?"

"You'll get another letter in your file. Tell about how you still have anger and impulse control issues, that kind of stuff."

"And? I have tenure; they can't take my job."

"No, not without a tenure hearing and that's not going to happen. But, they could make things unpleasant for you."

"Things are already unpleasant."

"They could get worse; they could make you go to anger management classes or something."

"I don't care. I'll take the letter in my file; it can keep the other ones company."

"Whatever you say, but I wish you'd reconsider. If you ever look for another job, your file will follow you. No one's going to hire you."

"That's okay. Where am I goin'? I've been here for thirty-six years; I'm just trying to make it to thirty-seven."

Chapter 48

Today's meet was the Clipper Invitational way out in Charlesport, a postcard-perfect seaside village on the west end close to an hour away. The Clipper was always fun because it was a good medal meet. With nice weather in the forecast, things were looking up.

The contrast between east and west end schools is pretty stark, mostly because of the differences in the communities. West end towns tend to be smaller and richer than their east end cousins. Even their names are nicer. Charlesport, Winslow Village, and Maple Hill sure sound better than Turndow, Rogers Depot, and Blattington.

The bus got to the school about forty-five minutes before the first event, but it took at least ten minutes to find the track. Charlesport's campus is so big that it looks like a college. First you turn off some Mayberry-type road like Hidden Creek Lane and go between these huge boulders that guard the entrance. Then, you drive on a private road for another half mile or so before you even see a building. The first one in sight is the field house, which has a full gymnasium, an Olympic-size swimming pool, beautiful locker rooms, and a state of the art weight room. Westfield is just like it – except that it doesn't have any of those things. Westfield High School sits directly on Front Street, a busy road that has trucks and vans zooming by all day. There's also Roosevelt International Airport a couple of miles away with the school directly on the flight path. The planes fly so low that the kids can wave to the pilots. Needless to say, the noise is deafening. Here, there is no noise except for the chirping of the birds.

Then there was the matter of their track. A brand new, garnet Mondo number, lined in white to reflect the Clippers' colors, glistened with dew in the morning sun. The field event areas were perfect too, with freshly painted lines, new pits, and sugary white sand for the jumpers. Just off the far turn, a garden hose gurgled gently as it filled the steeplechase pit.

Westfield's track was brickyard hard and so full of potholes that Wildcat runners had to memorize which lanes to avoid; that was their closest thing to a home field advantage. There was even a tree limb that overhung lane six on the second turn. If you were taller than about five-eight it could take you out, and more than one opponent had learned that lesson the hard way. Fish kept saying that he was going to cut the branch down, but he never seemed to get around to it. The field event runways were hard, cracked and faded, and there was so little sand in the pits that unwary jumpers tended to bottom out on landings, like boats run aground. Last year, things got so bad that Fish gave the entire team a weekend assignment.

"Over the next couple of days, go to the beach, fill up some buckets with sand, and bring them to practice on Monday," he ordered.

That's how the pits got filled. For a steeplechase course, there was a wooden barrier that Mr. Morrison, the shop teacher, had made for Fish as a favor. The course was still three barriers and a water jump short, but they weren't there so it didn't matter; Fish made do with what little he had – that was the Westfield Way.

So, everyone thoroughly enjoyed the good weather and gorgeous facilities of the Clipper, and had a reasonably good time. Frankie managed a second in the highs and a third in the intermediates, and Cam went home with gold in the 200, silver in the 400, and the phone number of a pretty Haitian high jumper from Greenmont. Everybody teased him about fraternizing with the enemy but he just laughed it off and said, "Gwaan, itz ahl good."

"Hypno Avi" went off by himself for a half-hour before his race to get his mind right, and Fish had about three coronaries trying to locate him, but he eventually showed up at the starting line on time and proceeded to run his best time of the season.

When he climbed up on the second rung of the medal stand to collect his silver in the mile, Pell whispered, "He still looks like a fuckin' zombie."

But Fish, echoing Clark Gable, said, "Frankly, I don't give a damn. He's our zombie and he just ran his ass off. We could use some more fuckin' zombies who can run like that."

Oscar closed the show with PR's in both throws, adding two more bronzes to his burgeoning collection. It was only about two weeks since he had started his diet, but the pounds were beginning to melt off. He was a good ten pounds lighter now and noticeably quicker in the circle. He was also starting to feel better about himself. While the other weight men were scarfing down hot dogs and sodas for lunch, Oscar sat contentedly with his back against a chain-link fence munching on an apple and drinking a diet Coke. He had even taken to wearing Under Armour now, in tribute to his new physique. He still looked like a sausage, but it was definitely a lower-fat sausage. The only bad thing was that "El Terremoto" had lost a few points on the Richter Scale.

Chapter 49

Avi and his wacko almost-a-friend Benjamin had decided to celebrate the weekend and Avi's fine finish in the Clipper Mile in their usual raucous Saturday night style.

First they stopped by Karl's Komiks to peruse the latest in comic chic. After half-an-hour of vainly searching for anything involving Wolverine or Magneto, Avi yelled out, "Ben, come here; I've been looking for this forever." Under a stack of old *Mad* magazines he had found an early '80's copy of Captain America that was in perfect condition. He grabbed the comic, gleefully plunked down seven bucks, put his treasure in a plastic bag since it had started to drizzle, and carefully slipped it inside his green Westfield windbreaker.

Then the lads were off to White Castle for the Daily Double – four belly bombs, two medium fries, and a chocolate shake each. With the current twin bill at the ancient Westfield Cinema featuring a *Star Wars* duo of *The Phantom Menace* and *Attack of the Clones*, Avi and Benjamin were looking at a good four hours of nerdvana.

It was while walking down Cedar Street on their way to the theater that Avi realized that things might not be so great after all. A navy blue, late-model BMW slowly circled the block twice and then eased ahead of them before neatly slipping into a parking space about half a block down.

Avi didn't like the looks of it but he kept his mouth shut, and Benjamin was too engrossed in thinking about the movies to notice what was going on. When three hulking teens wearing blue and cream Kingsbridge varsity football jackets got out of the car, Avi knew they were in for it.

Crossing the street to avoid a confrontation only delayed the inevitable. Two of the Kingsbridge guys jogged across the road to cut off their escape, while the driver hopped out of the car and came up behind them.

"What's up numb nuts?" the first jock greeted them. "Topher" was written in script on the left side of his jacket and the letters FB were emblazoned on the right sleeve.

"Out for a little Saturday night fun?" he teased.

"No, no, nothing," Avi mumbled as he backed away. "We're just g-g-going to the movies."

Benjamin, now that he'd finally figured out what was happening, had turned white as a ghost and was too petrified to open his mouth. It was obvious that he wasn't going to be a whole lot of help in this situation.

"What's playin' *Revenge of the Nerds*?" the second hulk, a bruiser named Geoff, taunted. "You jerk-offs should be starrin' in it, not seein' it."

"We d-d-don't want any trouble, we're just going to the m-movies," Avi tried again.

He was shaking a little now, but he tried not to let anyone see it.

"Don't be rude, dork," the first guy advised. "We just want to make sure you're safe; there's a lot of bad guys out tonight."

"Hey, what's that you got in your jacket?" Geoff asked, pointing a fat index figure at Avi.

"Where?"

"In your jacket," he repeated. "Clean the shit out of your ears."

"N-Nothing," Avi said.

"Right there," he said, poking Avi in the chest for good measure.

The cellophane wrapper crinkled when he touched it.

"I think you're hidin' something in there," he singsonged. "Let's take a look," he ordered, as he pulled the comic out of Avi's jacket.

"Wow, *Captain America*…my favorite," said Topher, as he snatched it from his friend's hand and slipped the comic out of it's wrapper.

"D-Don't, please," Avi pleaded. "I j-just bought it."

"Great, then it's nice and new. I just want to look at it; I'll give it right back – promise."

Instinctively, Avi grabbed for it, but a beefy hand belonging to the Kingsbridge guy behind him smacked him in the head and deposited him on the sidewalk. He found himself looking up at the sneering trio of bullies surrounding him.

"You know what, nerd? I really don't want to read this shit," Topher announced. "Here, you can have it back."

"T-Thanks," Avi said .

A wave of relief washed over him as he climbed back to his feet and reached for the comic.

"In two pieces," Topher snarled as he ripped the comic in half. His buddies were laughing hysterically.

"Or maybe in four," he corrected himself, as he ripped it again.

He tossed the tattered pieces in the street, and the three Kingsbridge guys sauntered off laughing and punching each other in the arms.

Avi just stood there; he was shaking with rage as the cold night wind blew the torn bits of paper all the way down Cedar Street.

Chapter 50

Fish had already relieved Matty of his slingshot, but he hadn't talked to him about it yet. So, after dinner was over and the older kids had gone off to finish their homework, he walked Matty out to the backyard.

"You know I had to go to your school again on Friday, right?"

"Yeah"

"I mean I had to leave work to go see Ms. Hazelton."

"I know."

"You know why?"

"Because of my slingshot?"

"Yeah, because of your slingshot."

"But, I wasn't doing anything bad."

"The principal said you were shooting at the girls."

"I didn't hit any of them."

"But you were shooting at them."

"No, I was just shooting near them."

"Near them?"

"Yeah, to scare them."

"Were you trying to hit them?"

"No!" Matty said indignantly.

"Could you have hit them? I mean, if you wanted to?"

"Sure"

"How about the other two times this happened? Did you hit anybody then?"

"No"

"Are you sure?"

"Yeah, I could've hit them if I wanted to, but I didn't. Especially Kara Brodsky – she's got a giant butt."

Fish stifled a smile as he slid the slingshot out of his back pocket. You had to give the kid points for honesty.

"Can I have it back?" Matty asked hopefully.

"Not yet," Fish answered. "But, I want to see something first."

"What?"

Fish pointed to a maple sapling about two inches thick on the far side of the yard.

"Can you hit that little tree over there?"

The target was a good twenty yards away.

"Sure, that's easy."

"Let's see it then."

Taking the slingshot from his father's outstretched hand, Matty pulled a smooth rock the size of a large marble from his jeans pocket.

"Geez! You always carry your ammo with you?"

The towheaded eleven-year-old grinned and then quickly fit the stone into the leather strap. Grasping the wooden handle firmly, he extended his left arm to full length and pulled back hard with his right hand. He paused in the ready position for a split-second and then let fly.

"Whap!" The sapling quivered noticeably as the stone struck it dead center about four feet from the ground.

"Nice shot! Can you do that every time?"

"Yeah"

"You're sure?"

"Yeah"

"Positive?"

"Yes!"

"How do you know?"

" 'Cause I practice."

"OK, then; let me have that slingshot back."

Chapter 51

It was another Blue Monday, and the last dual meet of the season was on tap against the pathetic Rogers Depot Engineers who hadn't won a meet all year. Then again, Westfield hadn't either so it looked like a toss-up. Since the meet was at home, the guys set up the track and then adjourned to the locker room for the usual pre-meet briefing.

"All right, everybody listen up. This is it, our last chance to get a win. I won't lie to you; Rogers Depot isn't real good and that's an understatement. They only have a couple of decent kids. They're very weak in the distances, and they don't even have a vaulter. They haven't won a dual meet all year, so we don't want them breaking their streak against us. Some of you guys have been coming along pretty well, some of you…uh…a little slower - but today's the day we put it all together. We need everybody involved, everybody contributing – not just five or six guys carrying the load. OK then: one-two-three, Westfield."

The team echoed the cheer and burst onto the track where the mighty Engineers were waiting – all fourteen of them.

"Geez! Where's the rest of their team?" Fish mumbled under his breath.

But there was no answer. The Engineers' coaches were on the far side of the track, and the few athletes they had were busy stretching and getting ready Most of them had headphones on anyway, so it's doubtful anybody was even paying attention.

"Well, at least we should get a win," Pell offered.

"Should," Fish responded. "But what would it mean? These guys won't even cover all the events."

Fish was right; Rogers Depot was pretty bad and they didn't cover all the events, but that didn't guarantee a Wildcat victory.

It's tough to win a dual meet without having scorers in every event because if a team is void in one area all its opponent has to do is put three kids in there. Then, as long as they don't get disqualified, they take all the points. If that happens more than once or twice, it's a done deal.

Rogers did it three times. They entered no one in the mile, two mile, or the vault, so the meet started off twenty-seven to nothing. But the kids that Rogers did bring were better than expected. They went one, two in the 100, scored in the 400 and 800, and surprisingly grabbed second and third in both hurdles. When they dominated the jumps, even the distance runners' earnest efforts and Oscar's stellar weight work weren't enough to secure a lead.

Fish looked worried as he and Cahill started planning the relays, but then again he always looked worried at track meets.

"You believe this shit?" Fish muttered. "We're gonna need two relays to win this thing."

"We're gonna have a problem then," Cahill replied. "We can't touch them in the 4 X 1, and we'll get the 4 X 4, so it'll all come down to the 4 x 8."

"Why's that a problem?"

"Because we're pretty much out of runners."

"How can that be? Who's left?'

"Simmons and McDermott can run, but they're hurtin'. They already ran twice, and I don't think they can handle triples."

"How about Avi?"

"We didn't give him his usual two-hour advance notice, so he'll freak for sure."

"He's a freak anyway – run him. Who else do we have? We can't lose to Rogers."

Cahill looked stumped, but then he smiled.

"How about Greenie, he's fresh?"

"Greenie? A half?"

"Yeah, he can make it. At least we won't have to worry about him staying in his lane. He can run all over the track; there's no rule against it."

That much was true, so after Cam, Russ, Kavi, and Frankie won the first relay, and Rogers ran away with the second, the law firm of Simmons, McDermott, Glick, and Green took to the track with the meet on the line.

Rogers was anything but a distance power, but they did have two respectable half–milers. They ran them first and last, with two back-up guys handling the middle legs.

Fish decided to run Simmons and McDermott one-two followed by Avi, who was already into his third anxiety attack of the day. He couldn't trust Avi to run last because he might suddenly decide at the last minute that he didn't want to win, so Greenie would have to anchor.

The gun sounded and Andy Simmons took off like a flash. Tired as he was, he opened up a quick lead and then held off a late Rogers challenge to pass the baton about five meters in front.

Steve McDermott's leg was a carbon copy of Andy's. Going out hard, he opened the lead further and hung on when the Rogers runner, who was as every bit as exhausted as Mac, couldn't catch him on the last straightaway.

Avi took the baton and immediately slowed down. After graciously letting the Rogers kid catch up, Avi kept him company for the rest of the first lap and part of the second. With the coaches screaming their heads off at him to open up, Avi finally got the message and picked it up. When he completed the final handoff, the team had a good twenty-meter lead.

Now it was all up to Greenie. Everybody knew that he got confused about lines and lanes in the sprints, but there was nothing to worry about here. He could run all over the track, as long as he didn't interfere with anyone. Not ever having run a half before, he went out way too hard, but the coaches had anticipated that. Coach Olson had stationed himself on the backstretch, so when Greenie came by he yelled at him to slow down. This command went either unheard or ignored, because Demond actually sped up, rocketing to a thirty and then a forty-yard lead.

As Greenie powered through the quarter, his teammates were in a frenzy. If he could just hang on for one more lap, they'd have their win. And then, something that no one could have ever imagined somehow happened.

As Greenie passed the finish line the first time, he seemed to forget that he had another lap to run. Instead of bearing left and running around the first turn again, he continued straight down the track, running about fifty meters past the finish line and into the chute that the sprinters use to slow down after they finish. Now he was totally lost – up the track without a paddle.

When the Rogers anchor runner saw what had happened, he got his second wind and blasted through the first turn while poor Greenie tried to figure out what to do. With Fish, Cahill and everyone else in green and white screaming at him, Demond became even more confused and cut across the narrow grass strip that separated the chute from the track oval in order to get back into the race. Since this was highly illegal, the finish line official immediately took off his hat to signal a disqualification. But, in a rare moment of lucidity, Greenie realized his mistake and decided that he'd better run back down the chute in the opposite direction, to get back on the track legally. While this was the right course of action, it took way too long. In the twenty or so seconds that he spent plotting his course, the Rogers runner pulled so far ahead that Greenie had no chance at all.

Demond gave it the old college try, but it was all to no avail. Rogers Depot took the race and the meet, sending their sad little band of ragamuffins into joyous convulsions. Our guys just milled around in utter disbelief.

Fish looked like he was about to be sick.

"Nice fuckin' job, Magellan," he yelled in Greenie's general direction. "I thought I'd seen it all," he continued, "but this takes the fuckin' cake. How can you get lost on a goddamn track? I swear it can't be done, but Greenie just did it."

You always hear about teams having these great, undefeated seasons, but Westfield had done exactly the opposite. They had just put one miserable, winless season in the books. The boys dragged away the equipment and slinked off the track. Nobody said a word.

Chapter 52

The coaches were huddled together before practice today, and Coach Olson, uncharacteristically, started the discussion.

"We finished oh and six in the duals," he began, "but I'm starting to think we can do something at Leagues."

"Not that old song again," Pell complained. "Do what? Finish last?"

"Do something good. You know, beat some people."

"You're nuts; you landed on your head too many times back when you were vaulting. "We lost to ev-er-y-bo-dy," he drew out the word for emphasis, "including Rogers Depot who sucks the big one."

"Listen, when we get to the championships we don't need depth, just some top-end stuff – which we have."

"You're startin' to sound like him," Pell said pointing at Fish, "which is never a good thing. And, for your information, we don't have enough top-end stuff."

"We could, if certain guys stepped up."

"Not happenin'! We are who we are, and our record says we're oh and six."

"Josh's right," Fish interjected. "We can do it."

"How?" Pell shot back. "How are we gonna beat six teams on the same day when we couldn't beat any of them the whole season?"

"Because, as I explained to you before, we don't need alot of scorers to win the league. If the top teams, say Kingsbridge and Greenmont, split points so that nobody runs away with it, and if some other teams, like Franklin North and Taneoke, chip in, we could find ourselves in a position to do something. What do you think, Kev?"

Coach Cahill slowly rubbed his chin and then pressed the palms of his hands into his temples like he had a migraine. He carefully considered the possibilities before answering.

"Could happen," he finally said. "But it's gonna take a whole shitload of things to go right."

"You're all fuckin' nuts. I'm the only sane one left – make me the head coach," Pell exclaimed.

"One more thing though," Fish added.

They all looked at him expectantly.

"What's that?" Pell asked.

"We still need a jumper."

Chapter 53

When Fish got home from practice, late as usual, his wife was waiting for him.

"We have to talk," she said.

"I don't like the sound of that," Fish replied dryly. "You really want that divorce? You know what they say, 'The first thirty years are the hardest.'"

"No, I don't want a divorce… at least not yet," she smiled. "I've spent too much time training you. I just want you to relax a little; you're killing yourself. You keep crazy hours, run around like a wildman, eat at strange times, and hardly sleep at all. It's not a healthy way to live."

"I've been doin' it for as long as I can remember. Why's it a problem now?"

"Because you have been doing it for as long as you can remember, and now you're fifty-seven years old with high blood pressure, and it's time to slow down. The kids and I really do want you around, you know. It'd be nice to have more time together."

"We do have time together. What about the summers?"

"The summers are great, but then August comes around and you're getting the cross country boys ready. Then it's indoor track and outdoor track, and the big invitationals for the really good guys, and then we do it all over again. It never stops."

"I'm not gonna do this forever," he argued. "A couple of more years. Then I'll retire from teaching, coaching, the whole bit. We can sit in our rocking chairs and sip iced tea on the front porch all day long. We'll go to the ice cream social at night."

"Don't you dare mock me," she warned. "That's not what I mean, and you know it." Lightning flashed in her jade green eyes. "I just want us to have a normal life, like other people, without track dominating everything."

"I was a coach when we got married; you knew what you signed up for," Fish said. "You knew about the long hours and the missed meals, and the times when I couldn't be there. I do my best, really; I don't miss that many things."

"No, but you do miss some things and we miss you. I worry about you; I don't want to be a widow in my fifties."

"Well, don't get your hopes up," Fish said sarcastically. "I'm not goin' anywhere. Look at me; I'm strong as a mule."

"And just as stubborn," his wife thought. But at least she was nice enough not to say it.

Chapter 54

It was seventh period and Fish was on his way to lunch. Since he was a creature of extreme habit, he had exactly the same thing every day: yogurt and lemonade. The yogurt flavor could vary, but it had to be Dannon's. The lemonade never varied; it was always the pink one in a can. Fish still carried a lean 165 pounds on his five-ten frame, only about ten pounds more than when he'd captained the team at Central State. He'd withstood the onset of middle age and decades of his wife's good cooking very well, and he wasn't about to blow it all on lousy cafeteria food.

Before he stepped into the lunchroom, already chaotic five minutes into the beginning of the last lunch period, he stopped by the Phys. Ed. office to look for Jimmy Tristano, a long-time gym teacher and Westfield's varsity football coach. Jimmy and Fish were buddies from way back and ate lunch together a couple of times a week.

Fish rapped on the office door and when no one answered, poked his head inside. It was empty. There wasn't even a class in the gym and certainly no Jimmy, but way over in the corner, alone at the far basket, stood a tall, black youngster whom Fish had never seen before.

He was standing twenty feet from the hoop, casually swishing shot after shot. Fish stopped counting after seven in a row. Then the kid nonchalantly jogged to the basket, jumped straight up, and dunked the ball with two hands. Fish's eyes opened wide. This young man was getting more interesting by the minute.

The teenager was unaware that anyone was watching, so Fish knew that none of this was for his benefit, but what happened next was still astonishing. Moving back to the three-point line, the youngster fired the ball down so that it bounced high off the floor and then off the backboard. While the ball hung in mid-air, he raced to the basket, exploded off the hardwood, caught the ball while spinning 360 degrees, and tomahawked it violently through the hoop.

Fish's jaw dropped to the floor. Glancing around, he checked to see if there were any witnesses, but no one was around. Turning back into the gym, he yelled.

"Hey! Wait up!

But the gym was empty; the kid was gone.

Chapter 55

Fish was standing outside Mr. Tristano's first period gym class at 7:55 sharp the next morning.

"A very strange thing happened to me yesterday," Fish told his old friend.

"What's that? You get laid?" Tristano cracked.

"No, that would only be strange if it happened to you," Fish shot back. "But, I did see a kid shooting baskets in here during seventh period lunch yesterday."

"So? That's not strange; the gym's always open lunch periods."

"This kid didn't miss."

"Now that's strange. That should narrow it down, too."

"He was also dunking the ball like Michael Jordan, only better."

"Tanganyika Smith III," Tristano said.

"Excuse me?"

"Tanganyika Smith III"

"Who the hell is that? The president of Tanganyika?"

"No, a new student here."

"And, you mean there are two other people in the world actually named Tanganyika Smith?"

"Apparently so. This one started here on Monday. He's a transfer from some place down south, Virginia I think."

Fish looked at his friend quizzically.

"And why didn't you tell me about him?"

"He just came in. I don't even have all his paperwork yet."

"You know anything about him?"

"Not much. He's quiet, hardly talks at all. Helluva athlete, though. We're doing physical fitness tests this week, and he's the best kid in the class by a mile. He's probably the best athlete in the school."

"What'd he do on the test?"

"Oh, just six-three in the sixty-yard dash – in his old basketball sneakers. And, ten-seven in the standing long jump."

"Ten-seven?"

"Ten-seven."

"That's ridiculous. Is he a good kid?"

"Seems to be," Tristano shrugged. "He changes and comes on time."

"Who's his counselor?"

"Digsby, maybe. Let me check."

Tristano rummaged through the debris on his desk before locating a copy of the kid's sign-in form underneath a couple of old Taco Bell wrappers. .

"Here it is. Yeah, Digsby. Why don't you go see him?"

"I think I will – like right now," Fish said. "Thanks, Jimmy. I may owe you one here."

"You already owe me plenty. And, Fish, one more thing."

"What's that?"

"The kid goes by Tang; don't call him Tanganyika, he hates it."

"Thanks; Tang it is."

Chapter 56

Fish didn't get to see Brian Digsby on Thursday because the guidance counselors were busy prepping kids for Saturday morning's SAT's, but he did get to him first thing on Friday.

"Morning Brian, got a minute?" he asked as he sauntered into the guidance counselor's office.

"Yeah, sure, Fish. What's up?"

"I've got to ask you about a new kid in school, he just…."

"Tanganyika Smith III?"

"How'd you know?"

"Because everybody's asking about him."

"They are?"

"Yep… and with good reason."

"What's that?"

"Well… he's kind of a unique case, to tell you the truth. Here, let me show you. This just came in yesterday," he said as he handed Fish a piece of white paper from the top of one of his filing cabinets. "It's his transcript from George Washington Carver High School in Fairfax, Virginia. Take a look at his grades first."

Digsby pointed to the left hand column of the transcript:
AP English – F
AP American History – D
Advanced Calculus – F

Honors Physics – F
French 4 – D.

"Those are his majors; he also got A's in Music and Gym. What does that tell you about him?"

"That he's consistent? He's got a zero point four GPA in his core classes."

"No, you know what I mean."

"Yeah, he's smart but he doesn't do any work."

"Right. And why doesn't he do any work?"

"'Cause he's lazy?"

"No, because his life's all screwed up. He was the class valedictorian going into this year; his IQ is 151, for Christ's sake. Let me read you some comments from his teachers."

"Duncan Masterson, his AP English teacher, wrote, 'Tang is undoubtedly one of the most gifted students that I have encountered in my twenty-seven years at Carver. He possesses an innate ability to understand and analyze complex literature that goes well beyond his years. And, he also writes with uncommon maturity for a high school student. Alas, it breaks my heart to fail him, but he leaves me no choice. He has cut my class repeatedly this quarter and has failed to hand in any of his assignments.' His other teachers said similar things."

"But, listen to Terrell Reed, his basketball coach," Digsby continued.

'Tang is easily the best athlete that I have ever coached. He led our team to the State Finals last year, averaging twenty-two points and eleven rebounds a game. He was also elected by his teammates to be our team captain and proved to be an excellent role model for all of our younger players. His work ethic was outstanding, and he never missed a meeting, practice, or game.'

"So, what do you think now?"

"I don't know," Fish shook his head. "Maybe he likes basketball. Why's he so screwed up?"

"The story I got is that his parents are in the middle of a nasty divorce and he got caught up in it. It seems like it got physical, too. The father started hitting the mother, and Tang jumped in to protect her. Then, when the father hit Tang, he decked his dad. The cops got involved, and everyone ended up in family court. The judge down there decided it might be a good idea for young Tang to live someplace else for a while, so he came up here to stay with his grandparents."

"And, they would be the first Mr. and Mrs. Tanganyika Smith?"

"They would."

"All right, then. Thanks, Bri; I owe you one."

Fish was saying that alot lately.

Chapter 57

Because Saturday was an SAT day there was no meet, but there was a practice after the test. With the upcoming track schedule getting lighter, only two tune-up meets remained before the league championships. That meant only three weeks were left to get in top shape and run as fast as possible. Some of the guys were improving, the better athletes anyway, and the coaches, probably realizing that the season was more or less lost, were at least trying to make things more enjoyable.

Today's practice was a circus. In ring number one, the shot area, Pell had his boys throwing small boulders backwards over a pole vault crossbar. He said that he'd seen it on a YouTube video and that these crazy Swiss guys did it after they'd had a few too many. With the bar set at ten feet, Oscar sent a twenty-pound rock flying up and over. He won a dozen Dunkin' Donuts for his effort and then graciously offered them to the other weight men. In the old days, he would have polished off the whole box by himself.

In ring number two, the long jump pit, Fish had half-buried a three-foot, inflatable plastic crocodile that he'd bought at the dollar store. The grinning green reptile lay in wait exactly seventeen feet from the takeoff board, its toothy snout aimed at the jumpers. Once they were warmed up, they had to "Clear the Croc" three times in a row. Failure to do so meant certain death, or at least a lap of the track. Between the laughing, the trash talking, and the lap running not much actual jumping took place, but at least they were having fun.

The sprinters and hurdlers were in ring number three, the track, and they had a special drill today, too. Coach Cahill was in charge since the distance guys were on the road, and both he and Fish had been stressing the need to relax when running fast, particularly in the long sprints and hurdles. As the runners were about to start a set of fast 300's, he opened up a bag of Wise potato chips. That was nothing unusual; Cahill liked his snacks. What was odd was that he gave each runner two chips. Cam immediately ate his and got Cahill's "death stare" in return, along with two new chips and a direct order not to eat them.

"Listen up," Cahill began, "you will now run 300 meters, from here to the end of the second turn, in no more than forty seconds. Stay in lanes all the way. You will then get four minutes of active rest between reps; that means jogging, and you will do two sets of three 300's each."

Frankie shot Cam a puzzled glance.

"What's the big deal?" he asked. "This doesn't sound that bad."

"One other thing," Cahill continued. "You will carry a potato chip in each hand. If the chips aren't broken when you finish the run, you can eat them. If even one is broken, the rep doesn't count – you have to run it again."

Now that still didn't sound hard, but in reality it was. The first two reps were easy enough, but by trip number three the chips had started to crumble. What happens is that as you get towards the end of the run, lactic acid kicks in and you start to tighten up. Your legs weigh a ton, your arms thrash around, and you feel like you're running in mud. Cradling the potato chips gently in your hands forces you to relax and to "run loose." Frankie and Cam were the only runners to get through the first set without breaking their chips, but Frankie lost his on rep number four, returning to the starting line with only a handful of crumbs. Cam, who was so smooth that you could balance a cup of water on his head when he ran and never lose a drop, made it through all six 300's and then clapped his hands in delight, accidentally demolishing his chips. Everyone pleaded with Cahill to make him run a penalty lap for chip abuse, but he just slapped Cam on the back and christened him "The Potato Chip Champ."

As they walked off the track, exhausted but laughing, Frankie turned to his buddy.

"You do know I'm going to beat you next time, right?" he needled.

"An jus' ow ya plannin' ta do dat?"

"I have a secret."

"Yaint got na secret. Ow's a leetle eye-talian bwoy like ya gwyn ta beat a proud black mon like me?"

"You'll see."

"Ah'll be seein' nuttin'. Yu'll be da one seein' – mah black arse all da way roun' da track."

"Pringles," Frankie said.

"Whad?"

"Pringles. I'll get Pringles; they're potato chips that won't break. That's how I'll beat you."

Cam just looked baffled and shook his head.

Chapter 58

Fish woke up early. With six days a week devoted to teaching and coaching, there was pressure to do everything else on Sundays. After riding his usual hour on the worn old exercise bike in the basement, he got the crew up, dressed, and over to church just in time for mass. Then the Fischettis sat down to breakfast.

Today's schedule was busier than usual. Maria had a science project involving pregnant fruit flies that would require both time and help; for good measure, she had to study for a math test, too. Matty had a lacrosse game in the early afternoon and a trumpet lesson at four. Plus, they were all due at grandma's house for dinner at five-thirty. There was also the matter of the Trackmobile, which was making weird grating noises and leaking a viscous brown fluid. All

Fish really wanted to do was kick back, watch the ballgame, and read the paper, but none of that was going to happen.

Crisis number one came when the fruit flies, which were supposedly anesthetized, came out of their slumber a bit early. Before Maria and her mother, who was riding shotgun on the project, could classify them, they buzzed off to parts unknown, scuttling all of the data needed for the project.

Crisis number two occurred when torrents of rain started falling at a quarter to two, fifteen minutes before the start of the first place battle between the league-leading Westfield Warriors and their arch-rivals, the Pine Grove Hornets. Although lacrosse can be played in all kinds of weather, the fields at Memorial Park had just been planted and the nervous park supervisor didn't approve of rabid ten-year-olds tearing up his sod. The start of the game would have to be delayed until the rain stopped, which led directly to crisis number three.

Which was, if the game started late, it wouldn't end in time to make the trumpet lesson, which in turn would be pushed back, thus delaying dinner. It was a three-car pile-up of time and events, and Fish didn't see any way out of it.

But then his luck changed. The rain stopped magically at two, allowing the teams to take the field almost on time. An hour and a half later, a happy group of Warriors emerged as seven to five victors, thanks to a certain blond midfielder's second-half hat trick. Herding the spectacularly muddied Matty into the wheezing Toyota, Fish blasted home and pulled into the driveway at exactly ten to four. Since Matty was way too dirty to go into the house, Fish decided to hose him down in the backyard from where the youngster's laughter and screams soon alerted his mother.

"What on earth are you two doing out there?" she called.

"Nothing, just cleaning up," Fish replied.

"He's killing me, mom. The water's freezing."

"Man up, kid. Big lacrosse star, huh? What are ya – afraid of a little water?"

"Stop dad! I'm not a man; I'm only eleven," Matty complained.

"Quit your bellyachin'. When I was your age, I was already married and had a job. Geez, I was supportin' a family when I was eleven."

"No you weren't."

"Yeah, I was. I had two jobs, actually. I had to support your mother and her whole family, too. They were very poor you know."

"You're lying."

"No I'm not. Scout's honor."

"You're not even a boy scout."

"Will you get him in here? He'll freeze to death," his wife pleaded."

"No he won't. He's already frozen. Besides, he looks like one of those aborigines from New Guinea or someplace – you know, those mud men. Get your camera – see 'The Wild Man of Borneo.' Besides, don't you want him to look nice for 'The Trumpeter Swan?'"

"Don't call Mr. Bateman that; he's very nice."

"I'm not sayin' he's not nice; it's just that he thinks the world revolves around trumpets and I'm pretty sure it doesn't."

"It's four o'clock; please get him in here."

"OK, mud man, go dry off and get some clean clothes." After an hour of trumpeting, during which the rest of the family embarked on a fruitless search for the fugitive flies, everyone crammed into the green Pathfinder, Mrs. Fish's car, and headed for grandma's.

When they were first married, Fish and his wife went to his parents' house every Sunday afternoon for dinner, but over the years it had become a less frequent occurrence. After Fish's father had passed away, they had revived the tradition for a while, but it had recently returned to being more of an occasional event. Grandma was becoming more forgetful and harder of hearing, and even basic communication had become difficult.

When they pulled up at her house, the front door was already open.

"Hello nice people...and you too, Angelo," Grandma greeted them.

"Hi grandma," the kids chorused.

"Come in, come in; let me have your jackets."
They settled comfortably into the old sofa and chairs in the living room where the décor hadn't changed since the Kennedy administration.

Grandma and her sister Josephine, who was visiting for a few weeks, brought out the drinks. There was soda for the kids and wine for the adults, along with a couple of trays of snacks. As the kids gobbled up the appetizers, the grown-ups gossiped about the holy trinity of Italian conversation: family, friends, and food. Then they all adjourned to the dining room for dinner.

"Mom, did you see they're having a big sale at Kohl's this week?" Fish asked, trying to start a conversation.

"A what?"

"A sale - at the store."

"Mail from the poor? No, I didn't see any."
Grandma's hearing had really gotten worse, and the kids were starting to giggle.

"No, No. They're having a sale… this week… at the shopping mall," Fish enunciated carefully.

"No, I don't think I got any mail this week," Grandma continued. "Maybe the postman is sick; it's that nice Mr. O'Rourke, you know. He's been our mailman since before your father died."

Pretty much everything was dated from Fish's dad's demise; it was nine years ago and provided a handy reference point for all things chronological. The giggling grew louder.

"Mom, Mr. O'Rourke's not sick. Even if he were, you'd still get your mail. They'd send a sub."

"He's sick because he worked in a sub? That's terrible. You know, alot of those boys who went off to war were never the same when they came back. You know your father was wounded in the war."

Fish did know that his father had taken a piece of shrapnel in the South Pacific and that he had been awarded a purple heart. By now, the kids' giggling had turned to outright laughter.

"Shhhh!" he glared at all of them at once.

"No, ma, I'm sure he's fine."

"Who's fine?"

"Mr. O'Rourke's fine."

"Mr. O'Rourke has to pay a fine? Why? Because he missed a few days of work? And, after he served in a submarine during the war? That doesn't seem right." Grandma was getting angry now.

"He's been a good worker for a long time," she went on. "No wonder so many of those post office people go crazy, having to work under those conditions."

The kids were crying by now. Heads had slumped into bowls of pasta and Matty was in imminent danger of asphyxiation by spaghetti, but grandma was on a roll.

"Just the other day I read about a mailman down in Texas or Arizona or some such place; maybe it was Oklahoma. He went crazy and shot seven people on his mail route. I didn't even know postmen carried guns, did you? Why do you think he did that?"

Fish gave up.

"I don't know," he said. "Maybe it was that 'neither rain, nor snow, nor gloom of night thing'; they have to work in all kinds of weather. Maybe that's why they all go postal."

Grandma looked a little relieved.

"Well, the weather here is getting nicer, so we probably don't have to worry about that," she said smiling. "Now, who would like some dessert?"

They finished the coffee and cake by nine and headed home. Another crazy week was looming.

Chapter 59

On Monday morning, Fish began the hunt for Tang Smith in earnest. Before school even started, he went down to the cafeteria where the early birds grabbed a quick bite before first period, but there were only a couple of regulars there. Walking to the gym across the hall, he peered inside but the place was empty.

He decided to look outside. Since it was a warm spring morning, maybe some of the kids were hanging out or copying homework by the big tree in the parking lot, but no one was there either.

With only a few minutes to get to class, Fish jogged back into the building and decided on a shortcut. If he hustled down the music wing and cut through the rehearsal rooms, he could take the back stairs up to the third floor and still beat his students to class. It was a tad hypocritical to yell at kids for being late if you weren't on time yourself. As he waved to John Brancaccio, the music teacher, he heard piano music coming from one of the back rooms.

"Franz Liszt?" Fish yelled.

"Nice try – Brahms," Brancaccio corrected.

"I knew that."

"No you didn't. What piece?"

"I have no idea, but whoever's playing it is really good."

"That's the *Piano Concerto Number One in D Minor* for your information, and you're right; the pianist is terrific. New kid who just came in, name of…"

"Wait! Let me guess."

"Go ahead."

"Tang Smith."

"How'd you know?"

"He seems to be the answer to every question lately. Can I say hello?"

"Sure, he's just finishing up. He's got class now, anyway."

They walked to the rehearsal room and Mr. Brancaccio cracked open the door.

"Time's up Tang. Got to go to class."

"OK. Thanks, Mr. B."

"I want you to meet someone, first. This is Mr. Fischetti; he's the English chairman and the track coach here."

"Hey, Tang," Fish greeted him. "Where'd you learn to play piano like that? That sounded great."

"Oh, my grandmother taught me. I just fool around with it sometimes."

"I saw you shooting baskets the other day, in the gym," Fish shifted gears. "You just fool around with that, too?"

"No, I play some ball."

"You play any other sports?"

"Football, 'til ninth grade. Then I stopped; my basketball coach was afraid I'd get hurt."

"So you stopped playing?"

"Yeah, I quit. I figured my future was in B-ball anyway. Not that I have a future now."

"Why's that?"

"No grades - anymore. I failed almost everything last quarter."

"What year are you in?"

"Junior"

"Seems a little early to throw in the towel. You want to talk about it? I might be able to help, but we've both got class right now. What are you doing for lunch?"

"Nothin.'"

"Good, then. Come on up to the English Office; it's room 301. I've got the food covered; I'll see you there."

Needless to say, Fish was late for his period one class.

But, at exactly twelve-twenty, there was a knock on the English Office door. It was Tang.

"C'mon in; it's open."

"Mr. Fischetti?"

"Yeah. Come in - and call me Fish – everybody else does."

"Uh, OK."

"How 'bout something to eat? Turkey sandwich all right?"

"That'd be great."

Fish had stopped by the cafeteria during period five and gotten the least offensive-looking sandwich he could find; the turkey breast with lettuce and swiss had won a very lackluster competition.

"So, tell me something about yourself," Fish started as he handed over the sandwich. "How'd you come to attend our fine institution?"

"Not much to tell. I was goin' to school down in Virginia, but now I'm stayin' with my grandparents up here."

"That's it?"

"That's it."

It was obvious that the kid didn't want to say too much about it, so Fish changed up.

"Tell me about your name then; that's a new one for me."

"Smith?" the teen deadpanned. "Nah, it's really common."

Fish looked up to see Tang grinning broadly. At least the kid had a sense of humor.

"No, really."

"Really, it is. Nah…I'm just joshin'. My great grandmother was from Africa. After she came to America and met my grandfather, they had five kids. Their first son was named Tanganyika, in honor of where she was born. After that, it just became a family thing. I'm the third."

"The kids ever tease you about the name?"

"Not since I beat up Rashad Williams in seventh grade. That put an end to it. I don't really like Tanganyika; it's too long, but Tang is fine."

"Then Tang it is."

"How about school? Mr. Digsby told me you were a great student until this year. What happened?"

"Just some stuff"

"What kind of stuff?"

"School stuff, family stuff, you know…stuff."

"How are you doing here?"

"All right, it's only been about a week."

"How are your classes going?"

"A little boring, to tell the truth."

"Too hard?"

"Too easy. I learned most of this stuff in my old school."

"I thought you were failing down there."

"I was, but I still learned stuff; I just didn't pass."

Fish decided to make his move. He could always find out how Tang was doing from his teachers.

"Listen, if you're not doing anything after school why don't you stop by the track? We've got a pretty good team," he fibbed. "We can always use another athlete, though."

"I don't know. I never thought much about doin' track. I don't really see the point in runnin' just to be runnin'."

"It's not all about running; there's jumping and hurdling, different kinds of things. I saw you dunking the ball in the gym the other day; you sure as hell can jump."

Tang stared off into space for what seemed like a full minute.

"Could I just jump? No runnin'?"

"No running except what's necessary to do the event? That could definitely be done. Come on down this afternoon and we'll take a look."

"I can't come today; I've got to take my grandma to the doctor."

"All right, tomorrow then?"

"Maybe"

"You know… colleges give scholarships in track, too. Not just in football and basketball."

"They do?"

"Yeah, they do – if you're good enough."

Tang's eyes opened a little wider. "All right, I'll try to be there tomorrow then."

"I sure as hell hope so," Fish thought.

Chapter 60

The next day, Fish sprinted out of his last period class about as fast as a fifty-seven-year-old English chairman can sprint. He wanted to be at practice early and he hadn't told anyone about his lunch date with Tang, not even his assistants. The whole thing was supposed to be a surprise. The only surprise, though, was that Tang didn't show up.

All through the stretching and warm-ups Fish kept looking around. Usually he was relaxed and joking with the guys, but today he looked anxious. The assistants gave out the workouts, and Fish started to walk around the track to make sure everyone got going. About halfway through the first set of 200's his face broke into that toothy grin. Loping across the field on the far side of the track was one Tanganyika Smith III.

He stopped just in front of Fish and said, "Sorry I'm late, coach; I had to go home to change."

Fish looked at the enormous blue and gold Lakers shorts and the gray XXL Georgetown basketball jersey that Tang had on and smiled. He also noticed the worn-out old pair of red and white Nike Hyperdunks on his feet that weighed a couple of pounds each.

Ordinarily, Fish would have said something smart-alecky like, "That outfit's OK 'cause we're gonna' play the Knicks in a few minutes, and you're all set," but this time he resisted the urge.

"That fine, Tang. We're just getting started. Why don't you warm-up a little. Then we'll go over to the pit and see what you can do."

The whole team was instantly aware of the newcomer's presence, so everyone kept sneaking glances as he got ready. Even if Tang was a total spaz he was still the kind of guy you wanted on the team just because he looked like an athlete. Standing about six-two, Tang was "split high" with long legs and a V-shaped torso. He carried about a hundred and seventy pounds on his rangy frame, with those long, ropey muscles that promised both speed and strength.

After Tang had stretched and jogged a little, Fish walked him over to the pit where the long jumpers were finishing their drills. They had their inflatable crocodile set up at eighteen feet today and were straining to clear it. One by one they took their marks, sprinted to the board, and failed miserably. Two guys hit the sand before the croc and two others landed on him, all resulting in "sudden death."

"C'mon, fellas," Fish teased. "Eighteen feet? I can piss that far."

The jumpers laughed, but it was only to cover up their embarrassment. Eighteen feet is no big deal for a decent high school long jumper, but none of these guys had ever gone much further than that in a meet so this was a tall order for them.

"Can I try?" Tang asked hopefully.

"Sure, do you know what to do?"

"Just run and jump?"

"You got it; just run and jump."

Tang retreated down the runway. Most jumpers use a starting mark about ninety or a hundred feet away to build up speed before the board, but Tang was only about half that far down the runway.

"Should I run fast?"

"Medium. Just try to clear the croc."

"Okay," Tang answered.

He started off slowly, took eight powerful strides to the board, gathered himself, and then rocketed off the ground. He was five feet high when he passed Fish who was standing by the side of the pit, and he still had two feet of clearance when he soared over the croc. He landed in an explosion of sand well past the smiling reptile and bounced up grinning.

The jumpers' mouths hung open and Fish was laughing.

"Was that good?" Tang asked.

"Not bad, not bad at all," Fish understated. "Let's put a tape on it and see what it is."

Coach Olson, who had wandered over to see what all the fuss was about, marked the break in the sand while Fish pulled the measuring tape to the board.

Everyone stared but no one spoke.

"Twenty-one feet one inch," Fish announced.

Cheers erupted from the jumpers.

"Is that good?" Tang asked again.

"That's fine, especially for the first day."

Fish laughed to himself as he walked back up the track. The school record was twenty-one nine.

Chapter 61

The coaches were huddled in the track office before practice the next day.

"I guess you found your jumper, huh?" Coach Olson began.

"Did you see that?" Fish asked, "That was freakin' unbelievable. Twenty-one one, before the board, on half an approach? And, he was wearing those heavy old clodhoppers."

"So, he has some potential then?" Pell cracked.

"Yeah, to be the next Olympic Champion. We've never had anybody here who could jump like that."

Cahill interjected, "So what do we do with him?"

Fish paused to think for a moment.

"If he stays out? Long jump for sure. High jump, triple jump, you name it. I'll bet he can run, too. You see the stride on him?"

"He could be the fourth leg on that mile relay," Olson added.

"If he's in shape. I have no clue about that."

Pell jumped back in. "We can find out easy enough. Why don't you have a time trial?"

"400 meters?"

"Why not?"

"I don't want to scare him off. Besides, I sort of made a deal with him."

"What kind of a deal?"

"A no running deal. I only got him to come out because I promised him he wouldn't have to run."

Everyone stared at Fish.

"Don't look at me like that. I thought we should hook him first; the only thing he was interested in was jumping."

They stared some more.

"All right… I get it. We're a track team; everyone's supposed to run. But you know what? He wasn't comin' out if I didn't promise. You think I screwed up? Maybe I did. Who's got a better idea?"

Nobody did, but it didn't matter. When practice started, Tang wasn't there.

The guys went through their paces, but there was no juice. Word of Tang's epic leap had filtered through the team and the school all day, and now everyone wanted to get a look at the phenom, except that he wasn't there – not until a quarter to five anyway.

Just as things were wrapping up, Tang sauntered in.

"Nice of you to join us, Mr. Smith," Fish greeted him. "I hope these practices aren't inconvenient for you."

Tang just laughed.

"Sorry coach; I was unavoidably detained."

"Were you now? And why exactly was that?"

"I was trying out for the school play."

"You were what?"

"They had tryouts for *Grease* today, and Mr. B asked me to try out."

"*Grease*? Let me guess; you got a part."

"The lead - I'm Danny."

Tang was grinning from ear to ear. Fish wasn't happy, but he was smart enough not to start an argument when Tang was so obviously pleased by this recent turn of events.

"Did anybody else try out?" Fish growled. "I thought you were just a piano player."

Tang laughed again; he was impervious to Fish's sarcasm right now.

"I'm not JUST a piano player," Tang replied. "And yeah, a whole bunch of guys tried out, but they weren't any good." Tang smiled, "They didn't have the moves."

"And you did?"

"Of course," Tang answered, as he suddenly moonwalked ten feet backwards while waving both hands to the assistant coaches who had gathered around.

Most of the team was watching by now, and laughter erupted when Tang started to dance. Oscar's boom box, which was usually tucked away after warm-ups, made a sudden appearance and out of the blue Michael Jackson's *Billie Jean* was blasting. Tang put on one of Avi's little white running gloves and started prancing around. He moved like he had no bones, and even Fish had to admit that the kid could really dance.

Pretty soon, everyone joined the party. First it was the sprinters who were always up for a good time, and then the crazy pole vaulters, with Howley leading them in weird gyrations. The distance guys were next, inhibited and awkward, but sort of dancing nonetheless. Then the girls' team joined in, which made everyone feel less gay, and then the hurdlers and jumpers got going. Oscar and the throwers were fashionably late to the ball, but they muscled their way into the middle where Oscar danced with Tang and threw in a few baby earthquakes for good measure. When Tang finished up by leaping to the top of the four-foot fence on the outside of the track and then backflipping off of it to finish in a split, everybody went nuts.

Fish just looked at Pell and laughed.

"You believe this shit?" Fish asked.

"Nope," Pell replied. "But, it's all good – everybody's happy."

"It's all very good," Fish agreed. "Now, all we have to do is teach this maniac something about track."

Chapter 62

The track and field education of Tanganyika Smith began in earnest the next day. With the first of the two tune-up meets coming up on Saturday, the coaches had about forty-eight hours to get their boy ready.

"First, I have a surprise for you," Fish told him.

"Thanks, coach. For getting the lead in the play?" Tang teased. "You really shouldn't have."

"I didn't. It's for looking like you might actually be able to jump."

Fish reached into his track bag and pulled out a pair of almost new blue and gold spikes.

"These'll make you run faster. They're my son's, but his season's over now so you might as well use them. See if they fit."

Fish had estimated Tang as a size twelve and his guess was right on the money.

"How do they feel?"

"A little tight, but good. They're light, too."

"That they are and they're supposed to be snug, just not too tight. Let me see."

Fish got down on one knee and felt for Tang's big toe. There was about a quarter of an inch gap between the tip of his toe and the shoe.

"Wiggle it," Fish ordered.

Tang moved his toe up and down; the fit was perfect.

"Coach are you proposing?' Tang joked, "because if you are, I have to tell you I'm really too young and I don't know how my family would feel about the whole race thing. You're not African are you?"

Fish shot him a baleful glance out of one eye.

"I'm proposing that you shut the hell up. Are you ever serious?"

Tang looked dejected, but only for a second.

"Nah, not really," he said. "That never worked for me."

"Well, try to pay attention for a couple of minutes. I want to get you some steps in the long jump so you won't foul on Saturday," Fish explained.

"What do you mean steps?"

"It's the number of strides you take to hit the take-off board. That's the white stripe painted on the runway near the pit. See it? You're not allowed to go over it."

"Can I step on it?"

"Yep, stepping on it is good because they measure the jump from where you land to the edge of the board nearest the pit."

"Then I want to be as close to the end as I can, right?"

"You got it. Run it backwards first. Take sixteen strides and then look down. There's a hundred-foot marker on the side of the runway; you should be somewhere around that."

"OK"

Tang put his left foot on the takeoff board and ran back up the runway. When he'd run sixteen strides he slowed down and looked at the ground. He was just past the marker.

"Where'd you end up?"

"About two feet past the mark."

"So what's your starting mark?"

"Approximately one hundred and two feet, three point seven five inches," he proudly announced.

Fish laughed again, "Don't be a wiseass."

"About one oh two?"

"Right again. You see, that calculus stuff is starting to pay off."

Then it was Tang's turn to laugh.

"All right, now, let's see if this works."

Fish pulled a roll of white athletic tape out of his pocket and threw it to Tang.

"Tear off a piece of this and put it at your starting spot," he instructed. "I want you to run full speed down the runway this time, but don't jump. Just run past the board; it's called a run-through."

"Run fast?"

"Yeah."

"As fast as I can?"

"Within reason. You still have to be able to jump."

Tang paused for a moment to study the board and then sprinted hard down the runway. With his new spikes he felt like he was flying, and after about six strides he was near top speed. Barreling down the approach, his sixteenth step landed flush on the board, two inches from the end.

"How was that?"

"That was great, about two inches left. Now all you have to do is jump."

"On Saturday?"

"On Saturday. Oh, and one other thing - you might want to get to your European History class a little more often. You're not in Kansas anymore."

'I'm from Virginia," Tang replied.

Fish was grinning at him now.

"Oops! *Wizard of Oz* reference; I get it." Tang was smiling now, too. "And, how'd you know about my European History class?"

"I know about everything."

"But, Mr. Emery is sooo boring. And, he's about a thousand years old. I think he was there for most of the stuff he teaches."

"Good. Then he can give you a first-person account of what really happened."

Tang was undeterred.

"'When Na-pol-e-on was ex-iled to the is-land of El-ba in eight-teen-thir-teen, I was on-ly in the sec-ond grade, but I re-mem-ber the cir-cum-stan-ces quite viv-id-ly.'"

The kid was spot on. He had Mason Emery, who was deadly dull and about ten years past his expiration date, down cold, even to the inflection, but that wasn't the point. With great difficulty, Fish suppressed a smile.

"I can't even stay awake in there," Tang went on. "I might slip into a coma."

"Doesn't matter. You still have to go."

"I'll try."

"Don't try - go."

"All right, I'll go. But if I croak in there it's on you."

Fish just smiled at him.

Chapter 63

Today was Mix-It-Up Day at school, a program sponsored every year by the Multicultural Club. It was supposed to teach students how to get along better and encourage them to hang out with people they usually didn't talk to, but it didn't always work out that way.

Westfield was so diverse that most kids didn't pay much attention to what nationality or religion someone was. They were used to people looking, talking, and dressing differently, and people were pretty good with that. Some kids still got teased of course, but it was usually for doing something stupid or lame. Avi, for example, got made fun of for his bad grades, his pimples, and his lack of success with girls, but no one ever made fun of him for being Jewish. And Oscar, even though he was looking a little sleeker, still heard a few cries of "Fatboy" behind his back, but nobody ever said anything about his being Hispanic.

Today everybody had to eat lunch in the cafeteria, which got the program off to a disappointing start. Hardly anyone ever ate there except for some freshmen and the kids who got free lunch tickets. Almost everyone else went out since there were a bunch of fast food places and delis right around the school. The Westfield Deli across the street was the most popular, and Domenic's Pizza ran a close second. Dom was a good guy who ran a student special every day, usually two slices and a soda for four bucks, which really packed them in. The Yogurt Hut was popular with the girls, and Oscar now, because it served low-cal stuff for people watching their weight, and the Burger King down the block also had a regular clientele. So it was basically an angry captive audience that filed into the cafeteria to get "mixed-up."

The guidance counselors and Senorita Lopez, the pretty Spanish teacher and Multicultural Club advisor, assigned the seating. Frankie was seated at a ten-person table that included two freshmen boys who never spoke, a sophomore girl who never shut up, and a Korean girl who didn't even go to Westfield but was visiting her friend who did. For some unknown reason, the friend was seated at a different table. Mr. Arnett, a half-senile algebra teacher, was the faculty moderator for the group and he was clearly in way over his head.

After about five minutes of dead silence, Frankie decided to help the old geezer out. He asked everyone to start one of the ice-breaking exercises they were supposed to do. Everyone had to write down on a piece of paper something they liked and something they didn't like about the school. Then the papers were shuffled in the middle of the table and everyone picked a different one. The responses, which were anonymous of course, were then read aloud. After that, people were supposed to discuss them. At the very least, it would kill the remaining thirty-eight minutes of the period.

One of the freshmen mutes went first.

"My favorite thing at Westfield is having nice teachers," he read in a monotone. "My least favorite thing is having so many tests."

"Okay," Frankie thought. "That was pretty harmless."

It had to be another freshman's paper because there were four of them sitting there like stones.

Another ninth grader read, "I like all the freedom we have here. I don't like getting so much homework."

"Better"

They did have more freedom here than in middle school, but so did the jailbirds in maximum-security prisons. And, they had more homework, too, which was why it was called high school. Maybe that could lead to something.

Blaine Jurgens, a wise-guy junior who was always clownin' around, was up next.

"My favorite thing at Westfield is Avi Glick," he snickered. "My least favorite thing is that he never even talks to me."

Everybody cracked up, including the visiting Korean girl who may have only been laughing because everyone else was. Even Mr. Arnett woke up.

"You made that up," Frankie blurted out.

"No, I didn't."

Blaine looked annoyed.

"Why would I like Avi? I'm not gay! Look."

He passed the piece of paper over and it was true; that's exactly what someone had written.

The rest of the period was a blur because no one was really listening anymore and Frankie was busy trying to figure out who liked Avi or was just trying to be mean to him.

He studied the note again; the handwriting was definitely feminine and there were only four girls at the table. There was that very annoying tenth grader, the mysterious Korean girl, a hot-looking junior who had a boyfriend, and Natalie Carlson, who was a senior and had never shown an interest in Avi or any other boy for that matter.

The bell rang and mix-it-up lunch was over, but now there was a new mystery to be solved. Who was Hypno Avi's secret admirer?

Chapter 64

The next day was Saturday, and Frankie woke up to the sound of rain pelting off the window by the side of his bed. Not only was it pouring but it was blowing up a gale, too. He figured there was no way they were going to have a meet, but when there was no cancellation text on his phone, he grabbed his bag and set off at a jog for the high school. Sure enough, the familiar yellow school bus, Empire Transit 257 with Nicky at the wheel, was idling outside the locker room door.

Most of the guys were already on board, so Frankie took his regular seat in the back next to Cam who already had his headphones on and his eyes closed.

"Wa' happnin Rasta mon?"

"Gweh, Frankie; don' tak ta me. Ah gotta belly-ache dat's killin' me."

"That's all that hot shit you're always eatin'," he said rather unsympathetically. "What'd you have for breakfast – jerk goat?"

"Nah, din't 'ave nottin'."

Cam reached into his pocket and pulled out a piece of half-eaten ginger.

"Even da gingas nah helpin'. An', hit's rainin' like maad. Dis'll be a nas-ty day."

The bus was headed to the Red Raider Invitational at Redding, only about twenty-five minutes away, so for Cam's sake the ginger had better work fast. The rain started to let up a little, and as soon as everyone was on, the bus pulled out. There was only one bus now because there were only thirty guys left. The coaches had cut the squad down after the last dual meet because there was no point in carrying twenty extra guys who would never get to run. Throughout the season, entries are unlimited; the coaches can put ten guys in an event if they like. But in the championship meets they can only enter three individuals and one relay team.

So, there was no real reason to keep the extras; that's why they were all gone.

For the majority of the team this meet was about sharpening up, but it was also slated to be Tang's coming out party. Most guys would be nervous before their first meet, especially since it was so late in the season and raining too, but Tang seemed oblivious. He was just sitting calmly in the front, opposite the coaches, listening to his I-pod.

Everybody else was in his usual spot. Oscar was in the last seat on the right because it was a little bigger and he needed the room. He was busy munching a granola bar and playing a video game with Kyle Leclair, one of the other throwers. Avi was in the middle someplace with the rest of the distance team. He was deep into some sci-fi comic featuring mutants and aliens – par for the course. The rest of the guys were either sleeping or talking quietly. It was too early and gloomy out to make much noise.

When the bus got to Redding, it stopped at the far gate and the team trekked across the muddy baseball diamond to get to the track. Since there was no place to get out of what had now become a steady drizzle, the guys hunkered down under the wooden bleachers and tried to stay as dry as they could.

The first two running events were already called, so guys checked in and started to warm-up. The long jump, pole vault, and shot put were the first three field events, so those athletes got started too. Fish, who usually stayed at the top of the stands to coordinate everything, had abandoned his usual post. Coach Cahill had taken up that spot, while Pell headed to the shot and Olson to the vault. That meant that Fish had gone to the jump pit – no doubt to babysit Tang.

Frankie drew lane six, the outermost lane on the track, in the first heat of the intermediate hurdles. That was his price to pay for being good enough to make the first heat but not good enough to get a better lane. Of more interest was the fact that only two of the guys seeded ahead of him were in our league – Josef Danicic, the top seed from Kingsbridge, and Myles Brown from Greenmont. In lane six, your opponents can see you and you can't see anything. You're running blind until the second turn when everyone catches you because the staggers even out and they all run a shorter distance there. It's a fact that everyone runs exactly the same distance in the race, but it sure doesn't seem that way on the outside.

Anyway, Frankie took it out hard because he didn't want to get caught too quickly. At the halfway mark only the hard-charging Danicic had made up the stagger, but "Little Frankie" was already starting to tighten up. Forcing himself to relax, he pumped his arms to maintain tempo as a red uniform shot by on his left. With a hundred meters to go, he remembered the potato chip drill. He relaxed his hands and face, pretended to cradle a chip in each palm, and felt himself float towards the finish. Leaning hard at the line, he nipped the fading Brown for third.

When he climbed back up into the bleachers to get his time, Cahill gave him a thumbs-up.

"Not too shabby there, Frankie Boy," he said.

That was a good sign because Cahill could be a tad stingy with the praise.

"What'd I run?" Frankie asked.

"Oh, just fifty-seven five. That's a PR by what, a second?"

"Almost. Eight tenths, actually."

"Nice job!"

It had stopped raining now and the other events were in full swing. Positive reports started trickling in and the team began to perk up. With the bar at eleven feet in the vault, both Howley and Jakes were clean.

In a real shocker, Oscar's mother and sister had shown up at the meet too – minus Nando. Whether or not Oscar had even spoken to them since he left the house was an open question, but they were certainly here now. Even though they didn't know the first thing about track, they were watching intently from behind the shot circle and cheering wildly every time Oscar made a move. Although he was acting all cool and nonchalant, it was impossible for O not to notice them since they were the only people screaming at him in Spanish. Oscar had popped his first try well over forty-five feet, but he'd fouled by brushing the top of the toe board with his right foot. Undeterred, he put the next one out around forty-six and stayed in the circle, too. Beaming from ear to ear, Oscar waved to the crowd and then winked at his mother who smiled back. That toss put him in second behind Kingsbridge's Corneau who had all three of his marks over fifty.

The result we were really waiting for was in the long jump, but no news was coming. Cahill asked Frankie to run over there to see what was up, but when he got to the pit Tang was still sitting on the side listening to his music like he'd never left the bus. The event was moving right along, and Fish wasn't around either.

Frankie tapped Tang on the shoulder.

"Where's Fish?" he asked.

"I don't know. I think he went to the bathroom," Tang answered.

"Did you jump yet?"

"No"

"How come?"

"I'm in the last flight."

"What flight is this?"

Tang turned his palms up and shrugged.

"Well, we'd better find out."

Frankie found the official with the clipboard and very politely asked him what flight they were in.

"The last one," he said.

"The last one?"

"Ya got a hearing problem? That's what I just said."

Geez he was touchy. Frankie scooted back to Tang.

"Get up! Quick! You're up soon."

"OK, chill."

He got up slowly and touched his toes once or twice; Tang clearly wasn't going to get an ulcer over this. About then Fish reappeared, wiping his hands on a paper towel.

"Smith, you're up," the official bellowed.

"Showtime, Tang," Fish announced. "Just take it from that 102 foot mark."

The wind had died down considerably leaving just a hint of a tailwind. The best jumpers had been in the first flight and Tomas Danicic, Josef's twin, was the leader at twenty-two feet even. The last medal was sitting at twenty feet seven and with only a few of the lesser jumpers remaining things appeared to be settled; but Tang hadn't jumped yet. He was only in the last flight because he didn't have an official mark yet since this was his first competition.

He stood alone at the end of the runway with nobody paying much attention - just another kid in the last flight of an event that was taking far too long. But, that was all about to change. Tang shook out his arms, took one deep breath, exhaled, and then rocked into his run. He accelerated like a jet down the runway, his blue and gold spikes a blur as he hammered out sixteen perfect strides to hit the takeoff board an inch from the end. The sound of his left foot cracked like a gunshot off the board and everyone gasped as he soared up and out – past the seventeens, the eighteens, the nineteens, and the twenties. He flew past all the marks until he crashed back to earth in a great explosion of flying mud and sand. Shaking himself off, he took one giant step forward and made a ninety-degree left turn to exit the pit. Everybody laughed and then stared hard as the official pulled the tape

"Twenty-two feet eight inches," the official announced.

The crowd around the pit erupted, yelling and slapping Tang on the back, but he really had no idea why there was such a commotion.

"How was that, Fish? Was that a good one?"

"Yeah, that was a pretty good one. In fact, that's a new school record."

"That's the school record? Nobody ever jumped farther than that?"

"Nope. Never. You da man."

"Shoot," Tang grinned. "I shoulda tried this sport sooner."

Chapter 65

The next day was Sunday, the day that Oscar moved back home. That was probably a good thing, but who could be sure? Pell said afterwards that he and Frankie had given

Oscar a hand moving his stuff, but it hadn't taken too long because there wasn't much to move.

It seems that Oscar's mom had finally given Nando the boot after she caught him half-naked in his truck with Rosita, the little hoochie mama from down the block. And, with Nando out of the picture, now it was safe for Oscar to go home and be with his family.

When they were driving back home in Pell's old Dodge Dakota, Pell told Frankie that he was actually going to miss Oscar, even though he'd only been rooming with him for a couple of weeks.

"It wasn't so bad; ya know what I mean?" Pell said. "I mean, I hadn't had a roommate since college."

"Yeah," Frankie answered, "and Oscar's a good guy."

"He is, although I won't miss that damn music he was always playin'. It's gonna be a little lonely though."

"Maybe you should get another roomie," Frankie suggested. "You could advertise on Craigslist or something."

Pell thought about it for a minute and then shook his head.

"Nah," he said, "maybe I'll get a dog instead."

"A dog?"

"Yeah, to remind me of Oscar."

"What kind of dog?"

"I dunno, something big and sloppy. Maybe a sheepdog, somethin' like that. What do you think?"

"All right," Frankie responded. He really wasn't sure what the correct answer was supposed to be.

Pell turned pensive for a little while; then he snapped his fingers.

"I got it," he blurted out.

"Got what?"

"I know what kinda dog I want. What's that dog they use up in the Alps or someplace to rescue people?"

"Rescue people?"

"Yeah, like in avalanches or snow storms. They carry a keg of beer or something around their necks. Clydesdales?"

"No, Clydesdales are horses, like in the Budweiser commercials."

"Not horses, I'm talking about dogs - a big, shaggy dog."

"Like a Saint Bernard? They carry brandy around their necks."

"That's it; a Saint Bernard."

"That's a giant dog for an apartment."

"Not any bigger than Oscar."

"True."

"That's it then, a Saint Bernard."

Pell smiled all the rest of the way home.

Chapter 66

Frankie stopped by Fish's office as soon as he got to school. Usually they just talked track or maybe about the Mets, but Frankie wanted to fill him in on Mix-It-Up Day and Avi's secret stalker. Saturday had been too hectic with the meet and the weather and all, but right now seemed like a good time so he knocked on his door and waited.

"It's open," Fish yelled.

Frankie stuck his head in.

"Fish, you got a second?"

"Yeah, sure Frankie. What's up?"

"I've got to tell you about something that happened last Friday."

"Yesss?"

"It was Mix-It-Up Day, ya know? And, at my table there was this girl who wrote a note about liking Avi."

"There was?" Fish seemed justifiably surprised.

"Yeah"

"A girl?" Now he was incredulous.

"Yeah, a girl."

"Who was it?"

"I don't know."

"How can you not know? This is huge. How many people were at the table?"

"Not too many – like ten."

"How many girls?"

"Four"

"Can you eliminate anybody?"

"Well, there was Natalie Carlson, but I don't think she's into boys."

"All right"

"Then there was this junior chick who was pretty good-looking, but I think she goes out with one of the football guys."

"That's two down."

"There was also a sophomore girl who never stopped talking, but she seemed like a total ditz, not the type who would even notice Avi."

"And?"

"And some Korean girl who I don't think even goes to this school. She was just there because she was visiting somebody and they stuck her at our table."

"Do you know her name?"

"No, Chin or Chan or something. She had a name tag on but I couldn't read it."

"I'll bet the guidance counselors know who she is."

"Why would they know?"

"Because any official visitor to the school has to sign in at the Guidance Office. What do you say we do a little detective work?"

Fish grabbed the receiver off his desk phone, punched three numbers into the keypad, and waited for someone to pick up.

"Hey, Ada? This is Fish. Maybe you can help me out with something. Did we have a student visitor to the school last Friday? A Korean girl possibly visiting her friend? Yeah, I'll hold."

Fish turned to me, "She's checking; this should be quick."

A moment later I heard a voice on the line.

"Yeah, I'm still here," Fish said. "Very good, Choon-he Park?" C-h-o-o-n-h-e? I got it. And she was visiting whom? Jin Lee? Yep, I know her; she's in my journalism class. Yes, verrry nice girl. Thanks so much. OK. Bye-Bye."

"You got it?" Frankie asked.

"I got it."

"Who is it?"

"Jin Lee"

"Jin Lee likes Avi?"

"Evidently"

"So who's the other girl?"

"Choon-he?"

"Yeah, who's she?"

"She's Christian."

"Christian? I thought her name was Choon-he." Fish could be really confusing at times.

"Her name is Choon-he; Christian is a character in *Cyrano de Bergerac*. It means that Choon-he is speaking for someone else – in this case, Jin Lee."

Chapter 67

With one more tune-up on the schedule, Saturday's Pirate Invitational at Parkview, the coaches continued fine-tuning the guys they needed for Leagues.

It was amazing how much progress the team had made, but the record didn't show it. While the boys hadn't won a single dual meet, their improving performances in the Saturday competitions had them psyched for a good showing down the stretch. It also meant that only about ten guys would do the heavy lifting. More would be entered, but they really weren't going to matter much.

The emphasis was on speed training now. In the early season, when the weather is bad, runners concentrate on strength. But now, when the days are warm and dry, speed is what they need. So, practices had gotten shorter and even more intense.

Today the workout was running all out 150's. That meant that six sprinters and hurdlers filled all the lanes and basically blasted around the curve and down three quarters of the straightaway before easing up. Then they would jog slowly around the far curve and up the straightaway back to the starting line. There were exactly two minutes allotted to complete the recovery jog and then it was off to the races again.

The first group included Frankie, Greenie, Cam, Russell, Ronnie Echeverria, and Tang. The coaches had decided not to traumatize Tang by having him try a quarter so soon. Instead, they put him in the fast group for the first four 150's. They figured that they could gauge his speed against the other sprinters and also get a look at his natural endurance based on how quickly he recovered. He balked a little at first, reminding Fish about his no running promise, but when Fish told him that the speed work would help his jumping, he reluctantly agreed to give it a try.

On the first whistle, Greenie and Cam quickly grabbed the lead. Frankie wisely tucked back a little, figuring that Fish probably had a whole bunch of these in store for them. The others lagged behind until we got to the top of the curve. Then, Tang took off. He was in lane three, so he had a good look at everyone, but the truth was that he could have been running on the pavement outside the track for all that it mattered. He blew down the straightaway passing everybody easily except for Cam.

Most of the time you can feel a runner gaining on you, so you have a chance to gather yourself to hold him off. But Tang moved so suddenly and with so much power that he caught everyone by surprise. Only Cam caught a glimpse of him out of the corner of his eye.

Now Fish hates guys racing in practice. He says that it doesn't prove anything because you never go as hard as you do in a meet. And, he doesn't want anyone getting hurt when it doesn't count. But Cam had way too much pride to just let this newcomer go by. So when Tang pulled alongside, Cam accelerated, forcing Tang to push the pedal to the floor. True to his word, Cam did have another gear left and the two of them flew down the track, elbow to elbow and stride for stride.

The coaches didn't even yell to stop. They were as mesmerized by the battle being waged as everyone else. At the 150 mark Cam and Tang were dead even, but instead of pulling up they kept on going. They charged around the curve and up the far side to the 300-meter mark where Coach Olson made a half-hearted attempt to flag them down.

With 100 meters left in the lap, Cam's training kicked in and he opened up a slim lead, but Tang never backed off. He stayed right on Cam's hip until they crossed the finish line. The coaches' mouths hung open. Cam was already a fifty-flat quarter man and everyone knew he could go faster. If Tang could run even up with him, with no training whatsoever, how fast could he go?

Chapter 68

Fish knew that Avi was running better and stopping less, but there was still more in there. If he could get him totally untracked, there was no telling what he might do. So, after his morning journalism class had ended, Fish asked Jin Lee to stick around.

"Jin, I have an assignment for you for the next issue of *The Roar*," he began.

The Roar – otherwise known as "The Voice of Westfield High" – was our school newspaper and Fish, in addition to his other duties, was the advisor.

"Yes?"

"Yeah, we need someone to write a feature article on the track team. It'll be on the second sports page. You know, not too long – maybe around 300 words."

"Sure," the ever-agreeable Jin answered. "What should I write about?"

"That's up to you, but features work best when the subject is interesting. Pick something that the kids don't already know about, as long as it's related to the team."

"I could write about our mascot," Jin proposed.

"You could, but we actually ran an interview with the Wildcat last year."

"How about an article on the coaches? Coach Pellegrino is funny; he makes everybody laugh."

"That he does, but you'd have to clean up the language a little."

"I would have to clean up the language alot," Jin giggled.

"How about a feature on one of the runners?" Fish asked slyly. "We have a bunch of guys who've really improved this year."

"Like Cam? He's really fast."

"Yeaaah, but Cam's always been fast."

"How about Frankie? He's the captain."

"Frankie is the captain, but everybody knows about him; he's been on the team for four years. We need somebody that no one knows about - someone who's good but quiet about it."

Jin's face suddenly brightened.

"How about Avi? Nobody knows about him?"

"Avi?" Fish grinned mischievously. "That's a good one. How'd you come up with him?"

"I don't know. He just… popped into my head." Jin was blushing now, so Fish decided to let her off the hook.

"OK, then, Avi it is. You'll have to interview him. Can you do that?"

"Uh huh."

"All right. Set it up ASAP and we'll get it in the next issue. We go to press next week."

Chapter 69

The next morning, Jin was lying in wait for Avi when he got to his locker just before first period. She had prepared a list of thirty questions, enough for three features, and she was ready to start, but Avi was a somewhat less than willing subject.

"Hey, Avi," Jin greeted him. "I have to interview you for the school paper. Is that cool?"

"Me?"

"Yeah, you. Can you fit me into your busy schedule?"

"Why me?"

"Because you're only one of the best runners on the track team, that's why. Is it okay?"

"I am?"

Avi was totally immune to flattery, probably because he couldn't even recognize it, but Jin pressed on.

"That's what Fish said, and Frankie, too. Don't you believe me?"

"You talked to Fish and Frankie about me?"

Avi was having some serious trouble with the whole interview concept.

"I did. And, they both thought you would be a good feature for *The Roar*."

"Me?"

Avi had now answered every single question with a question of his own and the bell for first period was about to ring. Jin knew that if she didn't make her move now her quarry would escape and the interview would never happen.

"Listen, why don't we have lunch today? I can meet you period seven in the cafeteria."

Just then, the bell sounded.

"Uh, I gotta go."

"Avi?"

"I'm gonna be late for class."

"Please?"

"Um… OK. What period?"

"Seventh."

"Where?"

"Duh, in the cafeteria. So we can have lunch – and I can interview you?"

"Today?"

"Today."

"Okay."

And with that, Avi turned and ran off to class – much faster than he really had to.

Chapter 70

Today's practice was notable for two reasons: it seemed as if Westfield might finally have a decent mile relay team and Avi was running faster than he ever had before.

At the start of the workout, Fish handed Frankie a baton and put him with Cam, Tang, and Greenie to run a few variable-speed quarters. The idea was to run the first turn under control and then blast the middle 200. After that the runner could ease off and stride the last straightaway before passing the baton to the next guy. There were only six reps, pretty much all out for the timed 200's and just finishing easy.

Frankie was the leadoff man because Fish said he was the only one he could trust not to get disqualified. That was sort of a left-handed compliment, but it was basically true. Cam would have been a great first leg but he had to be saved for the anchor. Tang, fast as he was, was so raw that there was no telling what he might do; plus, he had never used starting blocks or run a real race. Greenie, as he had proven so often, was a very loose cannon. Although he was as quick a starter as anyone on the team, he was truly an excitable boy. In the mile relay only the first leg has to stay in his lane; after that it's a free-for-all. With Greenie and Tang running second and third, they could run wherever they wanted as long as they didn't interfere with anyone.

And, recalling Demond's disaster at the Rogers Depot meet, Fish added drily, "I'm pretty sure that Greenie can count to one."

It sounded like a plan and Saturday was the day to try it, so the boys got their sticks down and vowed to give it their best shot.

Avi was a revelation. The distance guys were running a middle-distance breakdown, and today that meant they would run 600-500-400-300-200-100, all fast and all on fairly short recovery. It was a tough workout, but this late in the season they had to go fast and they had to run tired. It was a good way to prepare them for the big races and the tough doubles and triples to come.

Now, Avi had been improving lately, and he seemed, with the help of his friendly neighborhood hypnotist, to have gotten at least some of his demons under control. But Jin's interest in him had completely altered his psyche. Suddenly, he seemed invincible. He blew through the workout, leaving his teammates breathless and his coaches speechless. He wasn't even sweating or breathing hard when he finished, while everyone else in his group had collapsed on the track ready to puke. Pell strolled over from the shot put area where he'd been watching and winked at Fish.

"Ah, love is a many splendored thing," he cracked.

"It's the April rose that only grows in the early spring," Fish sang back.

"He looks incredible."

"That's not the next line, but he certainly does."

"You think this is all Jin Lee's doing?"

"No, it's all the other girls chasing him around school - especially those pesky supermodels."

"No, really. What's going to happen if she doesn't talk to him after the interview?"

"Why wouldn't she talk to him? She likes him, and he's a nice enough kid – if a bit odd."

"I'm just sayin'."

"Don't worry about it."

"What if they have sex?" Pell asked. "He might break the world's record."

"Yeah, for the world's quickest sex act," Fish shot back.

"No, he might run even faster."

"Or, he might quit the team and kill himself because there'd be nothing left to live for. Anyway, I don't think we have to worry about that. Jin's not that kind of girl…and Avi's definitely not that kind of boy."

"I'm just sayin'," Pell repeated.

"Don't," Fish warned. "You'll jinx it."

Chapter 71

Jin Lee's interview of Avi had gone beautifully. In fact, it went so well that their conversation spilled over into eighth period and made both of them late for class. It didn't take long for the guys on the team to get wind of Avi's new friendship either. When they started ribbing him, he didn't even seem to mind much. At least he was getting teased for something good this time.

"Avi mon, hoo's da liddle Chinah dal' ya bin 'avin lunch wid?" Cam started.

"She's not Chinese," Avi blushed. "She's Korean. And, we weren't having lunch."

"Sure looked like lunch to me," Simmons chimed in. "You two were sittin' verrrry close."

"It was an interview."

"Yamon, ifin ya say so," Cam cackled.

"We're just friends; it was for the newspaper."

"Yah, yah, yah. I kin see da 'edline naw. 'Avi n' Jin ta Wed - Reveren' Fish Pree-siden.'"

A good-sized crowd had gathered now, laughing good-naturedly at Avi's distress and eager to pile on.

Oscar piped up next. "Are you guys plannin' a big wedding? I could be the best man."

"Only if everyone else was dead," Howley yelled, as everyone cracked up.

"All right, everybody listen up," Fish's voice cut through the din. "I don't know exactly what you're all doin', but I'm pretty sure it has nothing to do with track, so let's get started stretching."

Slowly, the guys broke into their groups and began to get loose. Then, Fish paused for a second and cleared his throat.

"And," he continued, "I just want to inform you that I am deeply honored and definitely available to officiate at the upcoming nuptials of Avi Glick and Jin Lee."

Everybody cracked up again – even Avi.

Chapter 72

The sun was shining, the bus was rolling, and the team was off to the Walter J. Prescott Last Chance Track Meet. The meet was held in honor of some local track coach who had died about twenty years ago, and it was called the "Last Chance" because it was the final opportunity for kids to get marks good enough to get into the championship meets. It was held at Bryantville High School, way out in the boonies, and was a team favorite because it moved fast. There were no heats or semis in the races; everything was a final on time. Even the field events were quick. There were three attempts in the long and triple, three throws in the shot and disc, and a five-jump rule in the high jump and pole vault. It all added up to about a three-hour deal.

Fish was using it as a dress rehearsal for next week's League Meet. Everybody was supposed to do exactly what he was going to do next Saturday so the coaches could get a good idea of where we stood. The only problem was that not too many other teams had shown up, so the meet ran even faster than usual. That made it seem more like a glorified dual meet than an invitational, but it was what it was.

The intermediates are always the first event and Frankie drew lane one. That was okay with him because at only five-seven on his tiptoes, he didn't have trouble with tight turns. And, the staggered start would force him to run hard to catch up. If a runner can make up the stagger by the time he goes into the second turn, he's in business. And, if he keeps pushing, he can have a nice little lead coming down the stretch.

The only flaw in Frankie's plan was that his opponents had no desire to let him catch them so quickly. When the gun went off, he went out hard and tried to cut down the stagger, but a red-clad Seaside guy in three and a black-uniformed Parkview kid in four were flying. After 200 meters of hard work he had actually lost a little ground, so he throttled back and settled in for the long haul. Around hurdle eight, though, a strange thing happened. The red guy who was leading slowed noticeably, took several tentative steps, and almost came to a stop before jumping the hurdle awkwardly. It was obvious that he couldn't hurdle with his off leg and he lost so much momentum that Frankie roared by him, along with the Parkview runner. As they headed down the final straightaway it was a two-horse race.

From the last hurdle to the finish line, the intermediates are all about being tough. Everybody's hurting and all form is shot to hell. Everyone's just trying to stay upright and finish strong. Frankie concentrated on keeping his head steady and pumping his arms as hard as he could. With twenty meters left he drew even and with ten meters to go he edged ahead. On the last stride he threw his arms back, dropped his chest, and dove for the line. Then he crashed to the track.

A second later Pell pulled him to his feet and people were pounding him on the back.

"Green one, black two," the head finish judge shouted.

"Sweet!" Cahill yelled from the sideline.

Even Fish was impressed. He sidled up to Frankie while he was still dusting himself off and whispered under his breath, "I never thought I'd say this, but you're beginning to resemble a hurdler."

That was Fish's highest form of praise and he made sure that no one else heard it, but Frankie knew what he meant. Four years of blood, sweat, and tears were finally paying off and Fish was proud of him.

His knee was bleeding from the scraping it took on his swan dive, but Frankie didn't care. He had a nice win and the 55.7 PR was gravy.

The meet was in full swing now, and guys were competing all over the place. Greenie was warming up for the 100 and Cam had his ear buds in, his sunglasses on, and his hoodie off, so he was getting ready, too. Tang had already taken a couple of jumps, narrowly fouling on a big one and then hitting twenty-one five on his second. Meanwhile, Avi was nervously pacing around and anxiously scanning the stands.

"What up, Mr. Av-ay?" Frankie needled as he sidled up. "Lookin' for someone?"

"No. Just lookin'."

He knew that wasn't true, so he kept on going.

"C'mon, you can tell me. Who's comin', Jin?"

"Maybe. She said she was gonna try and make it."

"Doin' another interview?"

"No! She just said she might come and watch. That's all."

"You want her to come?"

"No. I mean yes. I don't know."

Just then, Avi caught sight of a pretty Asian girl waving frantically from the far end of the bleachers. The lovely Jin Lee had arrived.

Avi's face immediately relaxed.

"All better, now?" Frankie asked.

"Yeah, no, I guess so. Leave me alone, will you Frankie?"

"Okay. Just don't forget you've got a race comin' up."

"I know, I know. I'll be ready."

"And, Avi, don't worry… you look pretty."

Avi stuck his middle finger up in the air, but at least he seemed less nervous.

The highs were coming up in about an hour and then the relay after that, but it was too early to start warming up, so Frankie wandered over to the concession stand to get something to eat and a bottle of water. He had five dollars in his pocket plus the twenty that Fish had slipped him with the usual instructions to "spread it around." Fish did this for every Saturday meet and the guys never knew about it. What he meant was that Frankie should make sure that some of the guys who didn't have much money, like Oscar and Cam, got something to eat and drink when they were done for the day. It was one of Fish's many little secrets and it sure made Frankie popular with the boys. Apparently, their captain was not only loaded but also quite generous. The shot put area was on the way, so it was a good time to stop by and check on Oscar, but the event hadn't even started yet. The officials and some coaches were arguing about the sector lines being too narrow, and the shot putters were just hangin' around talking and joking with each other.

The milers were on the track now, doing their strides and waiting to be called to the line. Avi was the fifth seed – partly because he had run some decent times lately and partly because there was a small field. Jin Lee was hanging over the fence at the top of the straightaway. How would her presence affect Avi? As far as anyone knew, no one had ever come to watch him run. His parents or siblings had never been at a meet, and the sci-fi freaks he hung out with at school were too weird to actually show up in public and cheer for him.

The gun went off and Avi immediately shot to the front of the pack. That was certainly a departure from his usual style which basically was to retreat and hope for the best. Even from 200 meters away you could see that he was going way too fast, and when he came by the first time Coach Cahill screamed at him to slow down and relax.

But there was no slowing down or relaxing. He shot through the quarter in sixty-one flat, a nice split if you were a world-class miler but a tad quick for your average high school distance runner. Fish and Olson were desperately trying to get Avi's attention too, but he was oblivious. Jin Lee wasn't helping matters either. Whenever Avi passed her she would let out a glass-shattering shriek and chant his name.

"Av-i! Av-i! Av-i!" she screeched.

This only caused him to accelerate more. With a maniacal grin plastered on his dopey face, Avi pulled thirty meters clear of the field and passed the halfway mark in a blistering 2:06.

The pace was suicidal, Avi had never even run a half that fast, but Westfield's little lovebird didn't know or care. He slowed a little on the third lap, but when he passed Jin Lee again he got excited and sped up some more. He came through the 1,200 meters in 3:16, still clinging to first, although his lead had shrunk to about five meters now.

As the runners hit the last backstretch, Avi started to fade. Truth be told, he had hung in there a whole lot longer than anyone expected and much longer than he should have. He was showing plenty of heart but very little sense. One guy went past him and then another, but when a third runner tried to pass, Avi held him off. As they turned for home, Jin Lee was in full voice.

"Av-i, I love you," she screamed. "I love you."

Even in his fatigue-induced delirium Avi heard those words, words that he may have never heard before or at least couldn't remember.

He straightened his back, quickened his stride, and sprinted hard with a tall blonde kid from Bryantville who was trying to get by him. In the old days Avi would have just given up, but now he went shoulder to shoulder with his opponent for the last 100 meters and never gave an inch. Just before the finish line he dipped his torso and squeezed in for third. His time – something around 4:26 - was a mere ten-second PR.

That pretty much answered any lingering questions about how Jin Lee would affect his running.

The bus ride home was a blast. Oscar got teased about taking so long in the shot that everyone had to wait for him, Tang for fouling on all of his long jumps except the winner, Cam for talking funny and stinking up the bus with his damned Jamaican beef patties, and Avi for his madcap race strategy and especially Jin Lee's exclamations of undying love.

When he got off the bus at the high school, the whole team made kissing noises and serenaded him with a chorus of, "I love you Av-i," causing him to blush uncontrollably and Fish and Pell to pound him on his fragile little back. With one more week to go, we were definitely feeling it.

Chapter 73

Every year, on the Sunday before the League Championships, Fish has a barbecue at his house. He invites all the coaches and seniors on the team to hang out, play ping-pong, and eat like there's no tomorrow.

The menu changed from year to year, but today it was chicken and ribs on the grill, with homemade potato salad and coleslaw. There was ice-cold lemonade to drink and Mrs. Fish's apple pie with vanilla ice cream for dessert.

Since it was always the highlight of the track team's rather limited social calendar, no one wanted to miss it. Frankie, as the captain, got there first to help set up, and the boys started filing in a half-hour later. Oscar was the next to arrive. Although the big man definitely wasn't eating like he used to, he still allowed himself an occasional indulgence and today was going to be one of them.

Greenie and Howley got there next with Demond's falling-apart wreck of a Honda Civic spewing fumes and belching smoke as he casually swung it into a spot directly in front of the house.

Cam dropped by a few minutes later, fashionable as always, in a green, yellow and black Jamaican-style shirt that had about a million tiny holes cut into it. When the early arrivals started kidding him, he rose up in mock indignation and declared,

"Gwaan, yah jus' jealous a mi cuz ya hain't got mah style. Ahm ah proud black mon an don' ya fah-get et."

Before the argument against him could gather any steam, Tang, who obviously hadn't gotten the memo that the party was "Seniors Only," strolled into the backyard clad in a bright red and blue dashiki that his grandparents had gotten in Africa. Everyone hooted and hollered and whistled at him, but Tang was unfazed.

"Behold the African prince," he solemnly announced. "Bow down before me and be eternally grateful that I have graced you with my royal presence."

Somebody made a crack about him looking like Prince Akeem in *Coming to America*, and Tang responded by laughing his Eddie Murphy laugh and bringing Greenie up to play the Arsenio Hall part.

Everyone was there except Avi, but Avi was always late so no one was too concerned.

"All right, everybody settle down," Fish started.

Howley was busy schooling Oscar in ping-pong, mainly because O hit every ball five feet off the table, but he held up his serve long enough to listen.

"I know you guys only came for the food," Fish chided, "but that means you gotta listen up for a minute. There's no free lunch here, or at least no free barbecue, so hold on. I know we haven't had a great season, but there's still time to do some good stuff."

Fish was standing on the little deck that was attached to the back of the house, which put him about four feet higher than everyone else. It was a good pulpit from which to address the crowd, and everyone had a clear view of him. They were all listening now. Even Fish's kids, who had wandered out from the house, started to pay attention.

"I just want to tell you that Westfield Track has been down for too damn long, and our time has finally come."

He sounded a little like one of those Sunday morning TV preachers from Tennessee or somewhere, and his face had taken on a pinkish hue.

"Amen, Brother Fish," Tang called out, but Fish paid him no mind.

"You have to believe in yourselves – right now - because if you don't, nobody else will."

The guys started to clap now, and Fish picked up the pace.

"Anything you can conceive, you can achieve, and I'm talking about winning a league championship next Saturday."

"Tell it like it is, Rev," somebody in the back yelled.

Fish was really into it now, sweating profusely and getting redder by the second.

"We've been waitin' a long time…a very long time…to make a championship run. It's something Westfield needs, something Westfield wants, and something Westfield deserves. I've been doing this job for thirty-somethin' damn years and I know in my heart that if you guys will just...."

And, with that, Fish gasped, clutched at his chest, and fell forward over the top of the cedar railing of the deck and into his wife's flower garden.

Pell and Cahill were the first to reach him. Olson called 911 while the coaches checked his pulse and breathing, and made sure that he hadn't broken anything in the fall. Fish was conscious, but he didn't look too good and he wasn't saying much. Everyone else just paced around nervously and waited for the ambulance to arrive. .

Five minutes later the ambulance got there, and the EMT's checked his vital signs before they put an oxygen mask on his face, strapped him onto a stretcher, and whisked him off to All Saints Hospital.

Coach Cahill, Mrs. Fish and AJ followed the ambulance in Cahill's car, and Frankie stayed at the house with the others to wait for her phone call. Maria was there to watch her little brother, and the track guys were all so shocked that they couldn't speak above a whisper. It sure seemed like a long time before the phone rang; Frankie grabbed it on the first ring.

"Frankie," Mrs. Fish began, "the doctors think he had a heart attack, but they're not really sure. They're going to run some tests to find out exactly what's going on." Mrs. Fish was talking, but it didn't seem to make much sense. Frankie couldn't get it all straight in his head. She had said something about Fish being "stable" or maybe "unstable;" he couldn't remember which.

Fish was indestructible; he never even got a cold. In all his years at Westfield no one could remember him ever taking a sick day. He had been absent once in a while, sure, but it was always for something else, an out-of-town wedding or a funeral or something. Not for being sick himself – never.

Frankie told the guys what he thought was up and Maria explained it to Matty, but everyone just wandered around aimlessly, too stunned to talk and too upset to eat.

After awhile everyone headed home. Coach Olson said that he'd text as soon as he knew something, and Coach Pell stayed at the house with Fish's kids. Frankie left after everything was picked up, and Pell promised to call him as soon as he could. Everything had been going so well, too.

Chapter 74

School was awful on Monday. Nobody could concentrate on anything and no one cared about anything except Fish getting better. Pell never called and he didn't respond to any texts. Either his phone was off or he wasn't checking it. Nobody wanted to call Fish's house either, because they didn't want to bother his wife and kids, and also because they might hear something they didn't want to hear.

So, everyone gathered up to practice at 3:15, still dazed by what had just occurred.

Coach Pell was standing at the locker room door, and he ordered everyone into the cafeteria. That was pretty scary and he didn't look too happy, but that wasn't unusual because Pell rarely looked happy. He had one of those faces that looked like it was made out of leather, and he always needed a shave, even if it was early in the morning and he had just shaved an hour ago. He was the only guy around with ten o'clock shadow.

Coach Olson was there too, but not Coach Cahill. That was too bad because Cahill was an ex-cop and if he were around it might have settled things down. At least people might've felt a little better.

"Fish did have a heart attack yesterday," Pell began. "They're still running some tests to see what the damage is and they'll let us know as soon as they find something out. Other than that, he's stable and resting comfortably, whatever that means."

"Can we do anything?" Oscar yelled from the back.

"Not yet. We have to wait and see what the doctors say. He might need a bypass, or a stent put in, or maybe nothing at all. We just have to wait."

"Can we visit him?" Avi asked.

"Maybe in a few days. Right now, it's immediate family only. We're still gonna practice, though. League Champs is Saturday and that's only five days away."

A collective groan went up.

"'Stead a practicin' on dis 'orrible day, p'haps we shuld ahl ga 'ome and pray for Mr. Fish's well bein' – each en 'is own way a causs," Cam offered.

"Perhaps you should get your lazy ass out on the track, shut up, and run," Pell responded.

"Dat's anutha way a lookin' at et," Cam grinned.

"Let's go then," Pell ordered. "Get changed and we'll get started."

Chapter 75

Fish was feeling a little better on Tuesday. The doctors had decided that there was no serious damage to his heart and that he could go home in a day or two to rest. Under no circumstances, however, was he going to be allowed to coach. He had to take it easy.

Coach Pell said at practice that some of the guys could visit Fish at the hospital tonight, and he suggested that just a couple of the seniors go for a few minutes so as not to overwhelm him. He put Frankie in charge of the operation and there was no shortage of volunteers for the mission. They finally decided to pile into Howley's father's old minivan for the trip to All Saints.

Howley drove and Frankie rode shotgun to navigate. Cam, Greenie, and Tang, who now called himself "an honorary senior" and had insisted on going, were in the middle row. Oscar took up most of the back row with Avi squeezed into what little room was left.

When the crew got up to Fish's room on the third floor, his wife was just coming out.

"Oh Frankie," she said, "how nice of you and the boys to visit."

"How's he doing?" Frankie asked.

"He's feeling better, thanks. He's still tired, though. I know that he's dying to see you boys, but try not to stay too long. He'll probably fall asleep on you anyway."

"We won't," Frankie assured her. "The guys just wanted to stop by and let him know we're thinking about him."

"Thank you so much; he'll appreciate that, I'm sure."

When Frankie eased Fish's door open, he didn't know what to expect. He figured there'd be all kinds of tubes and wires sticking out of him, but there was only an IV drip in his arm and a heart monitor going.

"Fish, you awake?" he murmured.

"Huh?"

"Coach Fish," Frankie whispered again. "Are you awake?"

Fish opened his eyes slowly.

"Well, I guess I am now," he snarled. "What the hell do you want? Can't you see I'm tryin' to get some sleep?"

He was smiling when he said it, so Frankie knew he was feeling better. Then Fish caught sight of the other guys - who had quietly slipped into the back of the room.

"Whatcha do, bring the whole goddamned team? I was just starting to enjoy life without them."

"Just some of the boys," Frankie answered.

"Oh geez! Who's here, so I'll know who to kill when I get out?"

"Rasta mon en da 'ouse," Cam yelled.

"Uh, I'm here too, Coach," Avi chimed in.

"Oscar esta aqui!" the big boy offered.

"And Howley, Tang, and Greenie," Frankie added. All of the visitors were present and accounted for.

"I sure as hell hope Greenie didn't give you directions," Fish said. "You'd be in freakin' Oshkosh by now."

Frankie had no idea where Oshkosh was, but he was pretty sure it wasn't anywhere close.

"And you Tang, what happened? You get a night off from singin' and dancin'?"

Fish never missed an opportunity to rag Tang about his part in the play, but Tang took it all in stride.

"No problem, Fish. I got it covered. Want me to sing somethin' for you? Maybe a lullaby? Put you right to sleep."

"God no!" Fish exclaimed. "Haven't I suffered enough?"

You could see by the sparkle in his eyes that Fish was delighted we'd all shown up, but he wasn't ever going to admit it.

"So, now that you're all here, what do you want to do, have a party?"

"Dat's a fine taught," Cam agreed. "Ah got da music right 'ere."

"I don't want to hear any of that reggae shit," Fish grumbled.

"How 'bout some salsa then?" Oscar suggested.

"How 'bout not?"

"Coach, we were afraid that you might need blood or something," Howley said.

"From you guys? Thanks, no."

"Why?" Avi asked. "Are you afraid of getting AIDS?"

It was hard to tell if Avi was serious or not; you never knew with him.

"No, I'm not afraid of getting AIDS," Fish replied sarcastically. "I'm afraid of becoming like all of you. Next thing you know I'll be eating ox tails and tacos, listening to rap music, and dating little Asian women."

Fish's eyes were dancing now and he was sitting up straighter in bed. You could see the energy coming back.

"Don't you people have homework to do or something?" he asked.

"Nah," Frankie said, "We're seniors."

"Besides," Greenie added, "I just got into UCLA."

"Yeah?" Fish snorted. "What's that? The University on the Corner of Lincoln Avenue?"

The intersection where Lincoln crossed Preston Street was a notorious hangout for crack heads, hookers, and winos, and even Greenie had to laugh. Fish was definitely back to his old self.

"Well then," he added, "if you folks are about through, why don't you all get the hell out of here; I've got to get some rest so they can wake me up later to see if I'm sleeping."

The guys filed out grinning; they knew that Fish was on the mend. Frankie was the last one out, and Fish was slowly sliding back under the covers as he quietly closed the door.

"Frankie," Fish called.

He turned around just in time to see Fish wink at him.

"Couple a days," Fish said. "Tell the boys…couple a days."

Chapter 76

School was back to normal today, which was good because it meant business as usual. Knowing that Fish was at least feeling better calmed everyone down, and once the visitors had debriefed for the team everybody wanted to know when the headman would return.

"Is he gonna be back tomorrow?" one of the anonymous freshmen asked.

"Nah, not tomorrow," Frankie told him.

"How 'bout Friday?" another inquired.

"I don't think so. The doctors aren't sure."

"But the League Meet's on Saturday."

"So?"

"So, he's gotta be back by then."

"He can't be back 'til he's better. The guy just had a heart attack; give him a break, will ya?"

These guys were definitely getting annoying. Some things were more important than track, right?

"All right knuckleheads, let's get started," Pell's voice boomed.

"Intervals all the way around. Last hard workout before Leagues," Cahill was talking now. "Not too many, but pretty fast. Sprinters got ones and twos – three of each at about ninety percent. Take three minutes recovery between. Middle distance and distance runners do a mile easy and then a six-four-three-two breakdown. We're really running today, so put some juice into it. Jumpers are with Coach Olson and weight men with Coach Pell. No finesse stuff today. Sticks, steps, and starts tomorrow. Got it? Let's go."

We had it and we went.

Everybody was running fast, "Like they meant it," as Fish liked to say. The assistants were doing their best, and the team definitely had a chance to do something at the League Meet. Now, if Fish could only be there….

Chapter 77

The good news came down about ten-thirty the next day. Fish was out of the hospital and resting at home. The bad news was that he was under "house arrest" for the immediate future and was to avoid all stress. The guys correctly deduced that coaching this particular bunch of clowns wouldn't pass inspection.

That meant that the looming challenge would have to be met without him. The other coaches could definitely handle the X's and O's; they could set the line-up, too. The missing ingredient was the motivational part. Fish knew how to push the right buttons. Some guys needed a pat on the back and others needed a kick in the ass. Some had to have everything spelled out for them and others just had to be left alone. Fish knew the formula – that was his gift.

Frankie saw Avi outside the gym at lunch. He was heading off to eat with Jin since they were pretty much joined at the hip these days.

"Hey!" Frankie called. "Wait up."

They slowed a bit until he could catch up.

"Where you guys going?"

"Just the deli," Jin offered.

"Mind if I tag along?"

"Nah, come on," Avi muttered. He looked a little peeved, but Jin was her usual cheerful self.

"What's the matter? Trouble in paradise?"

"No, nothing," Avi said.

"He's just upset 'cause I can't go to the meet Saturday." Jin explained. "I have to go to my aunt's house in the city for a birthday party. She's like ninety or something."

Now the problem was clear. Avi figured that without his muse present he wouldn't run well. All of his hard work would be for nothing, and he didn't want to let the team down.

"Can't you get out of it?" Frankie asked.

"I tried, but my parents are really old-school; family is everything. When I told them that I wanted to stay home to go to the meet, my father almost had a stroke. And I really haven't said much about Avi. They won't be thrilled that he's not Korean."

"Are you even close with this aunt?"

"Close? I've only met her like twice. The last time was when I was about seven."

"So, she probably wouldn't miss you all that much?"

"No, not at all. She's pretty out-of-it, too. I don't think she would even recognize me."

"And your parents won't change their minds about letting you stay home?"

"Not a chance"

"OK then…."

This could definitely be a problem.

Chapter 78

T minus one day - and counting. Tomorrow was the big one and the team still wasn't totally ready. Fish couldn't coach, Avi was all bent out of shape, and, oh yeah, the mercurial Tang had gone AWOL for the last two days and nobody had a clue as to his whereabouts.

Frankie asked Pell if he had any ideas, but the weight coach just shook his head.

"Face it, Frankie. Without everybody on board, we're cooked. We might be cooked anyway. We've got no margin of error at all on this thing. We need Tang to win the long and do some serious running, and Avi's the only distance guy we've got who can score real points."

"What else can we do?"

"Pray? Maybe it'll rain and the meet'll get pushed back to Monday; that would buy us some more time. I doubt it'll happen though; the forecast is pretty good – partly cloudy and in the seventies."

There was no real practice today. It was just some light stuff – going over the line-up, reminding guys what time the bus was, stretching, and getting loose.

Pell said that in order to win the guys would have to "hit everything," meaning that every projected point would have to come in. That's almost impossible to do in a track meet because there are so many events going on that it's not really feasible to have everybody come through at the same time.

Cam had to win the 200 and 400, Avi had to score big in the mile and deuce, Oscar needed to be no worse than second in both weights, and all three of our lunatic vaulters had to place in the top five. Oh yeah, Tang, if he even showed up, had to win the long jump, and Frankie needed to be first or second in both hurdles. And, Pell added, "It would really help the cause if we could win the mile relay." If all of those miracles came to pass, Westfield would have close to ninety-five points, or about twenty fewer than Kingsbridge figured to score. So, they had to screw up as well.

Practice finished up with some relay passes for all three teams, but nobody's heart was really in it. The euphoria of knowing Fish was feeling better was giving way to the realization that winning the League Meet wasn't about to happen. Even though the team had come a very long way since those first frigid March days, they were still, like everything Westfield, a little bit short. Pell was totally right; there was no room for error and there were plenty of pitfalls lurking. The guys grabbed their bags and headed out in a hurry. The bus was scheduled for nine o'clock tomorrow morning. T minus sixteen hours - and counting.

Chapter 79

The alarm rang at eight-thirty sharp, and Frankie cocked one sleepy eye open. There was no rain at all, damn it. It was a little overcast, but there was absolutely no sign of any precipitation. Breakfast was his usual pre-meet energy bar and Gatorade, and he caught the team bus about five minutes before it was ready to pull out.

"Everybody here?" Pell bellowed.

"No, Coach. Tang and Howley aren't here yet," somebody yelled."

Howley was perpetually late, and Tang hadn't even been around the last couple of days. He'd missed practice on Thursday and been absent from school yesterday. If something was up, the right thing to do was to let a teammate know so he could tell a coach. If something really drastic happened, the rule was to call one of the coaches directly on his cell, but that was reserved for life-changing events. So far, nobody had heard a word from Tang.

Howley came flying up on his bike, stashed it between the back door of the school and some bushes, and hopped onto the bus at exactly nine o'clock.

"On time… as usual," he announced.

"On time…for once," Pell responded.

"Anybody have Tang's number?" Pell yelled. "We gotta get goin'."

Cam called out, "Ah got et," and began dialing.

Everyone waited quietly. They all knew they didn't stand a chance without Tang, but they also had to get to the meet. Cam let the phone ring for a while and then snapped his cell shut.

"Bumbaclot! Nawon answerin' da ting."

"Gotta go then," Pell rumbled. "Let's go Nicky; let's roll," and with that the yellow school bus nosed slowly into the street.

A half-hour later the bus pulled up in front of the graceful white columns of Kingsbridge Academy. Thankfully, there were no offensive banners greeting the team this time, so the boys filed quickly out of the bus and headed straight towards the back of the building and the Royals' spotless new track.

Kingsbridge had gone all out in preparing for their annual coronation. Red, white, and blue bunting hung along the fence ringing the track, making the whole scene look like a World Series game at Yankee Stadium. That was sort of fitting because the Royals were the Yankees of our county, winning championships regularly while looking down on the peons they annually trampled. Anybody who dared to oppose them was just a petty annoyance on the way to their manifest destiny.

Everybody hated Kingsbridge and their snotty "Our shit don't stink" attitude, but nobody could beat them. And, it sure didn't look like anyone would be up to that task today. The team formed a circle to stretch, seniors in the middle, while Pell went over the last-minute instructions.

It seemed weird that Pell was talking because Fish was always the guy who gave the pep talks; the assistants would just hang on the outside of the circle to make sure everyone shut up and paid attention. Peering over Pell's shoulder,

Frankie noticed, far across the field, what looked like a wheelchair approaching slowly along the concrete path.

The person in the chair was way too far away to recognize, but as the chair got closer he could just make out a figure that looked like Fish sitting and what appeared to be Mrs. Fish pushing. The other guys hadn't noticed anything yet, so he didn't say a word.

Mrs. Fish parked the chair on the side of the track while the guys finished their preparations, and as soon as they broke the circle she pushed her husband out onto the field and into their midst. The reaction was explosive.

"Fish!" Oscar screamed.

"Fish is here," yelled Avi.

"Where the hell did ya think I'd be?" Fish barked. "You guys think I was gonna miss this little soiree?"

"You can't coach, though, can you?" Greenie asked.

"Not in this goddamned wheelchair, I can't." And with that, Fish put his gnarled, old, arthritic hands on the sides of the chair, scrunched up his face, and with great effort slowly pushed himself into a standing position.

He stuck his battered old Westfield baseball cap, his meet hat, on his head, and pulled the brim down low over his eyes.

"If I can climb out of this freakin' wheelchair today, when all the doctors said it would be weeks, then you guys can sure as hell win one little track meet," he said.

Everybody was staring now. They were still shorthanded, but at least they had their coach back. Maybe they could do this.

"All right, stop your gawkin'," he shouted. "Let's go! There's a championship to be won."

The whole scene was pretty amazing, but while Frankie was jogging around the track finishing his warm-up, there was another surprise. Tang eased up alongside him on the backstretch and elbowed him in the ribs. Needless to say, the captain was shocked.

"Where have YOU been?" he asked.

"Around. I had to take care of some business."

"What kind of business?"

"Family business."

"You better tell the coaches you're here; they think you're missing in action."

"Nah! Fish knows I'm here."

"How could he know? He was in the hospital."

"He knows; I called him the other day. He knew I was coming."

"Then why didn't anybody else?"

"'Cause Fish didn't tell them."

"Why not?"

"I don't know, maybe for the surprise. Now everybody's gonna be psyched. Fish is back; I'm back; everybody's back. And, I got another news flash for you. You know how Fish just now magically rose up out of that chair?"

"Yeah"

"Well that was some serious Oral Roberts miracle shit there, too."

"What?"

"He's been up and around for a couple of days. He just played hooky from school so he could make a grand entrance - like the Second Coming."

"Bullshit!" Frankie protested. "Fish wouldn't do that."

"Truth. When I was on the phone with him the other day, his wife yelled for him to come have lunch. He said,

'I'll be right there,' and then I heard footsteps walkin' 'cross the room."

"Maybe someone else was walkin'."

"Nah. It was him. I even heard the chair pullin' out from under the table."

"You sure?"

"Yep"

The meet got started, and things went about as expected. The intermediates were up first, and Frankie grabbed second place behind his nemesis Josef Danicic. Unfortunately another Kingsbridge kid got fourth, so after one event the Royals were ahead fourteen to eight.

With the 100 next and the field events just revving up, the coaches, except for Fish who was watching intently from the top of the bleachers, were running around frantically trying to cover everything.

Not much was expected from the 100, and not much happened. Greenie, who managed not to get DQ'd, finished fifth, behind two Greenmont guys and assorted other sprinters. Luckily Kingsbridge didn't score, so they only led by four, but Greenmont's one-two finish garnered eighteen points and they took over the lead. Beating one of those teams was tough enough, but beating both of them was going to be impossible.

The mile was the third event, and all hope was pinned on Avi – never a good strategy. And his inspiration, the lovely Jin Lee, was nowhere to be found. So, Avi, obviously in a lovelorn funk, took the race out way too slowly and, despite the screaming of the coaches, never got to running much faster. Kingsbridge's Healy won the race in a breeze, and his teammates, Connolly and Doran, or maybe it was Doran and Connolly, completed the sweep. Avi staggered home a badly beaten fifth, so that was a twenty-four to two hosing and the Royals now led by a staggering twenty-six points.

The sky was starting to cloud up a bit, but it was much too late to get the meet postponed. The only thing that could help now would be lightning, and although it was humid it didn't seem muggy enough for a thunderstorm.

The guys were doing well enough in the field events, but they weren't making any real headway. Oscar threw forty-seven something in the shot, but big Ryan Corneau went fifty-two nine and blew him away. That one-two finish was reversed in the long jump when Tang won at twenty-two low and Tomas Danicic finished a few inches behind, but two more events were off the table and the Kingsbridge lead remained unchanged.

The wind was blowing harder as the runners got ready for the 400 meters. Cam was definitely capable of winning it, but there were a ton of good guys in the race. What was needed was some help. If Cam could win and some of the sprinters from the non-contending teams, Taneoke and Rogers Depot to name two, could slip in ahead of Kingsbridge and Greenmont, this thing could get closer.

The help that came was very little. Cam did his part by holding off a long-legged Taneoke kid down the stretch to win the race, but nobody else broke in and Kingsbridge used its depth to take third and fourth. That was worth the same ten points that Cam had just scored. With another event gone, the margin held steady at twenty-six points.

And, that's when it happened. Out of nowhere, the rain began. What started as a drizzle turned into a downpour and the downpour soon became a deluge. The skies opened, the wind gusted, and a flash of lightning split the darkened sky. A deafening boom of thunder followed immediately.

"That's it!" the Head Referee yelled. "Everybody off the track – lightning in the sky."

Everybody was grabbing their stuff and racing for the safety of the school when Fish appeared like a ghost out of the mist.

"In the equipment shed, now," he ordered.

There was a large blue equipment shed adjacent to the track, the kind of place where the school kept the lawnmowers and grounds-keeping stuff.

As the guys ran for the shed, they saw Fish arguing with the Kingsbridge athletic director, some tall, aristocratic-looking dork who had once been an Olympic yachtsman or something. The AD was pointing at the school building and yelling something unintelligible, and Fish was pointing in the other direction, towards the shed, and shouting just as loudly. Because of the rain and thunder, and with all the kids running around and screaming, nobody had a clue as to what they were saying, but it looked pretty heated. About ten seconds later, though, the AD handed his keys to a custodian who unlocked the shed door and Fish led the team inside.

It seemed pretty strange to be in the maintenance shed when everyone else was in the school where it was warm and dry and there were bathrooms, drinking fountains, and actual chairs to sit on. The guys were sprawled out on lawnmowers, rolls of rubber matting, and bags of fertilizer. Water was dripping through the seams in the roof and it was so dark in there that Fish had to prop the door open to see. That let even more rain in and made everyone wetter than they already were.

Westfield was losing by twenty-six points, the guys were drenched and miserable, and they were sitting in a leaky, smelly, old equipment shed. What was the point?

"Gentlemen," Fish began, as he propped himself up on a hundred-pound bag of topsoil. "Do you know why we're sitting here in this goddamned, old, piece-of-shit equipment shed?"

Nobody answered.

"Because," he continued, "Kingsbridge won't let us in their building."

What? Everybody was staring at him now. What the hell was he talking about?

"You all saw me arguing with their big shot AD, trying to get you guys inside, right? You know what he said? He said, 'No room at the inn.'"

"I said, 'You gotta be kiddin' me; everybody else is inside. You gotta have room; I've only got twenty-five kids here.' That prick said, 'We can only use the back hallway; the rest of the school is off limits. And, the Fire Marshall won't allow any more people in the building.' That's what he said."

Everyone stared in disbelief.

"That's not the truth, though," Fish went on. "The truth is that he doesn't want Westfield kids in his precious building. Remember that sign the last time we were here? 'Kingsbridge Dumps Westfield Trash' or some shit like that? That's what they really think of us."

Nobody could believe what Fish had just said. Kingsbridge wouldn't let Westfield in their building? That was impossible; all the other teams were inside. Was this actually happening or was Fish just playing another one of his crazy mind games? And did it even matter? Even if he was making this stuff up, the gist of it was still true. Kingsbridge had always hated Westfield and Westfield had always hated Kingsbridge. That's just how it was and it wasn't ever going to change.

"We're good enough to work for them, to pick up their garbage and mow their lawns, but we're not good enough to go inside their school," Fish ranted. "You believe that shit? And you know what he really thinks...what they really think? They think that we'll never be good enough - that we don't matter. We're just Westfield - a bunch of low-class, no account immigrants whose great-great-great grandparents didn't all come over on the fuckin' *Mayflower*. They think, even though they'll never say it out loud, that we're just a bunch of stupid wops and spics and kikes and micks and niggers and every other damn thing that they can just piss on and roll over – AND THEY CAN'T!"

Fish was screaming now, and everybody was afraid that he was going to have another heart attack. The assistants were all trying to calm him down, but he was way past calming.

He was such a good actor that it was impossible to tell if he was lying or telling the truth, but there were tears in his eyes and a catch in his throat as thirty-six years of frustration and rage boiled over.

"Well, gentlemen, I don't believe any of it. And, I know that you don't either. So, just as soon as this track meet gets started again, we're going to prove to those pompous assholes, once and for all, that they're wrong - dead wrong. We're going to prove to them that... WESTFIELD...DOES... MATTER."

The sky was beginning to brighten and the rain was letting up, so the guys toweled off with some rags they found in the back of the shed and stormed out to their own personal version of Armageddon.

The meet picked up right where it had left off, and Fish's words had definitely helped, but the desired results didn't come. The high hurdles were the first event after the rain, and even though Frankie ran as well as he ever had, he couldn't catch J. Dan. That was another plus two for the Royals who now boasted a twenty-eight-point bulge. The 800 meters was a wash, with neither team scoring, and the 200 saw Cam nab his second gold of the day to pick up a couple of points, as Kingsbridge took third and fifth. That was a nice morale booster, but the gap was still plenty.

Then fortune smiled – three times actually. In the pole vault, the three amigos, no doubt inspired by Fish's fiery rhetoric, suddenly got excited and swept the event. Although Kingsbridge took fifth, Westfield had suddenly moved a huge twenty-two points closer. And, even though Tomas Danicic won the high jump, Wildcat athletes picked up enough garbage points there and in the triple jump to stay within shouting range. After Oscar finished second to Corneau again, this time in the disc, Kingsbridge's lead stood at eight with only the two-mile and the relays left.

Avi was anxiously pacing back and forth as the distance guys got ready. As Frankie jogged over to him, Avi's eyes, big as saucers, were frantically searching the stands, but Jin Lee was nowhere to be found.

"Avi, relax dude. It's going to be all right."

He didn't even answer.

"Earth to Avi, hellooo, can you hear me?"

Still nothing - nobody was home.

"Avi, your race is going to start. You might want to go to the line about now."

"Huh? Where?"

"The starting line – over there – where all those other skinny-looking nerds are standing."

Avi moved like a robot in one of those cheap sci-fi flicks, shuffling mechanically until he took his place towards the end of the runners in the front row.

The gun went off and he continued his tortoise-like pace. As Healy and the rest of Kingsbridge's Irish Mafia took it out, Avi stayed near the back, neither passing nor being passed, in a kind of Jin Lee-less netherworld where nothing had any meaning. He was immune to his coaches' pleas, his teammates' cheers, and his opponents' movements. And, this went on for lap after unending lap until there was just one circuit of the track remaining.

As he entered the first turn of the final lap, still trailing by a good fifty meters, a familiar high-pitched voice rang out.

"Run, Av-i, run!"

It was Jin Lee. Somehow she had gotten here. And standing right behind her were three guys nobody had never seen before, two young and one old, who looked suspiciously – right down to their black-framed glasses and yarmulkes - like the object of her affection. Could Avi's family actually be here? They didn't even know what track was, and since it was a Saturday shouldn't they be off praying or something?

When Avi heard her, and when he first caught sight of her pressed up against the fence on the turn, a startling change occurred. Shaking his head to clear the cobwebs, he snapped out of his stupor and took off like a shot after the leaders.

He was in eighth place now, but that was only a temporary situation. Powering around the turn, Avi quickly passed three tiring runners and churned down the backstretch. He caught the fourth-place guy, a little redhead from Franklin

North, going into the last turn and set his eyes on the three Kingsbridge pacesetters. They had slowed down considerably, thinking that a sweep was at hand and trying to save some energy for the relays to come, so they never figured on Avi making a run. He roared by them like a runaway freight train, albeit a scrawny, near-sighted one, and won the race going away. Healy struggled home second, but both of his teammates, stunned by Avi's furious finish, fell apart completely and finished out of the money. That cut the deficit to six now with only the three relays remaining.

The relays always close track meets, and these races would crown a champion. There was definitely a shot now and the guys knew it, but there was still more work to be done.

The 3,200-meter relay was first - four guys running a half-mile each. With all three of Kingsbridge's distance stars exhausted from the just finished deuce, and with Avi lying prostrate on the track with Jin Lee tending to him, both squads turned to their "Scrubinis," as Fish called them, to put points on the board. Westfield's reserves were just a little better than Kingsbridge's, or maybe not quite as bad, so their fourth place to the Royals' fifth narrowed the gap to four points.

The 400-meter relay was next, with both teams expected to finish well back. Form held as Greenmont's sprinters ran away with the race. Taneoke finished second, and Rogers Depot took third. With Greenie running a good leadoff and the wild and crazy vaulters handling the other legs, despite their inability to pass the baton at all, they grabbed a crucial fourth. Kingsbridge, in total disarray by now, finished sixth. That was plus three more points. Westfield trailed by one measly point now – with one event remaining.

The 1,600-meter relay, the truest test of speed, strength, and heart, would decide the meet. Amazingly, it had somehow all come down to this - one race - winner take all. Fish had his best team ready to go. Frankie would lead off, Simmons would go second, and Tang and Cam would finish it up. But Kingsbridge, at least on paper, was better. They would run the brothers Danicic, and the kids who had finished third and fourth in the individual 400.

Fish gathered the boys around, not that they needed any instructions at this point, to go over the strategy. That's when they all noticed that Andy Simmons wasn't looking too good.

"What's the matter?" Fish asked him.

"My ankle's killing me," Andy muttered. "I think I twisted it at the end of the 800."

"Why didn't you say something before?"

"It didn't hurt then; I was sitting down stretching."

"Can you run?" Fish asked. "Try a strideout."

Simmons tried to run, but after about three steps he looked like a car with a flat tire.

"All right – that's not gonna work," Fish declared dryly.

"Three minutes," the head official announced.

"Who gonna run wid us?" Cam screeched.

"Avi!" Fish hollered.

Avi?

"Bumbaclot," Cam reacted first.

"Fish, nothin' personal, but Avi's no quarter-man," Tang stated the obvious.

"And, he's out of it," Frankie said. "He's lying under a tree with his head in Jin Lee's lap. He may never run again."

"He will run again… in about five minutes," Fish said. "He's our only alternate – he's got to run."

"What leg is he gonna run?"

"Anchor"

"Anchor?"

"Nah, Mistah Fish," Cam protested. "Lemme run di anka. Dat Danicic's a rude bwoy; he be walkin' Avi dan like nuttin'."

"Avi's not ready to run yet," Fish explained. "If he runs last at least we can buy him a few more minutes. It won't be much, but it's the best we can do. Oh, and one more thing."

"What's that?"

"You guys better give him one hell of a lead."

Pell was still hoisting Avi to his feet and giving him the bad news when the starter called, "Runners to the line." Westfield had lane four, a good lane on the six-lane oval. Kingsbridge had a better one; they were in three.

The gun went off and Frankie took it out against Tomas Danicic, the kid who had scored so many points in the jumps. He was a strong runner, too, so Frankie tried to stay as close as he could for as long as he could. Coming around the last turn and into the homestretch, he gave it everything he had and closed to within a few meters, but Danicic passed off first, and Kingsbridge's lanky second man immediately moved to the rail.

None of the other teams had really seen Tang run before because he was always jumping, so when he blew past the startled Royal on the backstretch everyone assumed that he was just an inexperienced kid making his move way too early, but Fish knew better - Tang wasn't coming back. With his impossibly long strides, he flashed around the turn and into the straight opening the lead with every step. When he handed off to Cam the lead was close to twenty meters and the place was going crazy.

Most teams try to hide their slowest runner on the third leg and Kingsbridge was no exception, but Fish had put his fastest guy, his true anchorman, in the third spot. Cam took it out hard and then ran harder. Fish had said to give Avi a big lead and Cam was determined to do just that. He zipped around the turns, flew down the straights and handed off to Avi who had finally collected himself enough to make it to the passing zone and take the baton.

With a fifty-meter lead now and only one lap to go, the race should have been in the bag, but there were still a few problems. First, Avi was exhausted from his Herculean effort in the two-mile, and second, he had very little experience when it came to running quarters. To make matters worse, he didn't like pressure and there was a ton of it on his skinny little shoulders now. Finally, the Kingsbridge anchor, Josef Danicic, was a cold-blooded killer who had run down guys way faster than Avi. He had already won both hurdle races and he could probably run even up with Cam for a quarter if he wanted.

With the crowd screaming, the suddenly panicked Kingsbridge fans for the home team and everybody else for the gritty underdogs, Danicic went after Avi with a vengeance. He quickly closed the gap from fifty meters to forty and then to thirty. By the time they hit the last turn, the lead was down to twenty and shrinking fast.

Nobody wanted to think what it would be like if Avi got caught. So much had gone into this that a loss now, when there was a chance to pull off an upset for the ages, would be brutal. And, Avi would be scarred for life – if not longer.

He took everything personally; if he lost this one he'd have to be put on a suicide watch.

Avi's shoulders hunched and his stride shortened as Danicic closed in. The Kingsbridge runner smelled blood and the home crowd sensed it. Coming into the last straightaway, the longest 100 meters in the world, Jin Lee was pleading, both teams were screaming, and the crowd was roaring.

Avi's lead was down to five meters now, but Fish wasn't screaming at all. He had calmly moved along the backstretch of the track, about thirty meters past the first turn and directly opposite the finish line. He made the sign of the cross and then pointed his index finger at Pell who was about twenty meters in front of the finish line on the other side. Pell answered with the slightest of nods, and while it was impossible to tell exactly what was going on there was a quick flash of movement under the royal blue tarp that was draped over the hurdles to protect them from the rain.

As the flailing runners surged towards the line, Avi trying desperately to hang on and Jo-Dan, wearied from his huge effort, straining to pass him, they staggered in tandem.

One step from the line, with a photo finish looming, Pell reached down and sharply tapped the blue tarp. Imperceptibly, a small, perfectly round pebble rocketed from beneath the cover and struck Avi hard on his right butt cheek. He lunged forward suddenly, inches ahead of Danicic, and collapsed to the ground just past the line.

"Green, red!" the finish judge screamed.

Pandemonium followed! The impossible had happened! David had slain Goliath!

Everyone charged out onto the track, hugging and dancing and screaming and crying. Pell was bear-hugging Olson, Cahill was smacking Frankie on the back, Cam and Tang were dancing wildly with each other, Oscar was embracing his mother, Jin Lee was kissing Avi, and Fish was wandering around in the middle of it, taking it all in.

In the madness, no one noticed a tall, skinny, blonde-haired boy with a WHAM-O slingshot clutched tightly in his left hand as he quietly slipped out from under the royal blue tarp and quickly jogged away from the track.

Chapter 80

The next morning, Nina Fischetti leaned down and kissed her husband gently on the cheek.

"Wake up, champ. Rise and shine. It's almost nine-thirty, time to get everybody up."

Fish just mumbled into his pillow and turned over. Every bone in his body hurt and he had a headache, too.

"C'mon, get up," Nina persisted. "Don't you want everybody to make a big fuss over you at church?"

"Not really," he said. "I'm so beat I can't move."

"That's no way for the leader of the mighty Westfield Wildcats to act. Here, look at the paper."

She tossed the sports section of the *Westfield Gazette* to him and sure enough there was the headline:

Westfield Shocker
Underneath, in slightly smaller print, it read:
Winless Wildcats Take League Crown
It wasn't all a dream, Fish realized. It really had happened.

"So, what do you say, coach? Shall we go to church and meet your adoring public?"

"I dunno," Fish said softly. He was smiling weakly now, but mostly he just looked exhausted.

"What? On the day after the biggest win in Westfield Track history you don't want to bask in the glory?" his wife chided. "You must be getting old."

Fish grinned. "I think I am. Maybe you're right. Maybe it's about time to give it all up. This would be a good way to go out."

"Be still my beating heart," she scoffed. "You don't really mean that, even though I wish you did. You're just tired."

"Maybe," Fish conceded. "But, I think I've seen enough kids run enough laps around enough tracks."

"Let's go to church," Nina said. "I want to thank God for this sudden epiphany."

Epilogue

School was closed today because it was Memorial Day, but everyone was still celebrating anyway. It was the first and probably last time anyone connected with the team would ever experience anything quite like this, and nobody wanted to let the feeling go.

Fish was feeling better – the victory over Kingsbridge had certainly improved his disposition and he was getting stronger by the day. The other coaches were just happy that the long grind was over.

A few guys, Frankie, Oscar, Tang, Cam, and Howley, were going on to the bigger meets, Counties and States, but there was no chance for a team title there. Avi had qualified, too, but he was so fried, both mentally and physically, that he'd decided to bag it for the rest of the year. Jin Lee, whose presence had absolutely enabled Avi to run like he did, even explained how she'd made it to the meet.

After her parents had left the party, Jin had called her friend Choon-he, the girl who had been at Mix-It Up Day. Choon-he had hurried over and replaced Jin at the party, and Jin had hired a cab to get her to the meet. Sixty dollars later she was there.

"Didn't your aunt realize you were gone?" Frankie asked her.

"Nah, she never even noticed. Choon-he said she talked to Aunty for half-an-hour and she never knew. You know all us Asians look alike."

So what did it all mean? The guys had won Westfield its first track title in way too many years, but that really wasn't it. They had also done something that no one thought they could do, and that was closer to the truth. But what had really happened was that they had learned to believe in themselves. Oscar had found his confidence and become a young man. Tang had found a family and become a student again. And, Avi had found love and become…well…a slightly less anxious, fearful neurotic. Hey, you take what you can get.

As for Fish, in spite of his pleas to the contrary, he'll be back. And, Pell, Olson, and Cahill will too. Track is a drug – it's the crack of the sporting world and once you're hooked it's impossible to quit. Fish had been a "track head" for about forty years now so he wasn't going cold turkey anytime soon – not him or the others. And, despite his somewhat dubious methods, he had changed everyone and taught them the most important lessons in life. He had shown a whole town full of doubting Thomases that the impossible is possible, that miracles can happen, and that dreams do come true.

So, that's about it. As far as next year goes, Howley and Jakes are joining the marines. They want to be Special Forces guys and they're both crazy enough to pull it off. In fact, Howley already has a "Semper Fi" tat on his left shoulder. Greenie's heading off to good old Westfield Community College to study who knows what, although Fish did suggest Geography as a possibility. And Oscar's going there too, but at least he has a plan. He wants to study nutrition and then set up a bi-lingual diet center right here in town. It's really a pretty cool idea when you think about it; God knows there are enough porkers around to keep him in business forever. Avi wants to go wherever Jin Lee goes, but since her grades are so much better than his that might prove difficult. More likely, he'll end up at a college near hers and that should work out better. Tang's got another year left at Westfield and there's no telling what he might accomplish, but there's also the risk that he might chuck it all to go back to Virginia or to star in a Broadway musical or something. Cam just signed a track scholarship to the University of South Carolina. It's kind of far away, but his family doesn't have much money and it's a free ride to a real school. He'll major in PE down there, run like the wind, and no doubt break hearts all over the Southeastern Conference.

And then there's Frankie, the undersized hurdler with the huge heart who symbolizes everything that's good and right about Westfield. Even if he's not certain about what he's going to do this summer, he knows exactly what he's going to do next fall. He's going to college, to Central State actually - Fish's alma mater – to study Sports Management in their Business School. And, there's one other thing that he's absolutely, positively sure of: he'll run godammit – he'll run.

Acknowledgments

My first novel, *Fish*, took a mere forty-three years to write, so my next effort isn't due until 2058. Writing my book, however, was far from a solo effort. My sincerest thanks go to everyone who helped and inspired me along the way.

First and foremost is my wonderful family that supported me at every turn, and provided real-life models for several of the book's characters. My everlasting gratitude goes to: my wife Melanie, who is not only a great proofreader but as patient and perceptive as Nina Fischetti, my older son TJ, who helped greatly with the research, my daughter Jennie, who was my first reader and head cheerleader, and my younger son Mike, whose computer wizardry solved all of the book's technical problems.

Furthermore, many thanks go to: Cathy Poe, my high school English teacher and teaching colleague who has inspired me since 1964, Barbara Aronowitz, who taught alongside me for so many years and also served as the book's chief editor, Curtis Cornwall, the real-life Cam, who served as *Fish's* Jamaican dialect coach, and Frank Santora, my first track captain and long-time friend, who served as the model for "Little Frankie" Carbone.

Finally, "Go Wildcats" cheers go out to all of the Oscars, Tangs, Avis, Greenies, Jin-Lees, Pells, Olsons, and Cahills whom I've had the pleasure to teach, coach, and work with for lo these many years. Your stories could fill another book. Hey…there's an idea.

CPSIA information can be obtained at www.ICGtesting.com
Printed in the USA
BVOW06s1156100615

403999BV00024B/601/P